Alice Returns

Through The Looking-Glass

ZIZZI BONAH

All characters in this story are the creation of Zizzi Bonah, (with exception to the character of Alice, who was created by Lewis Carroll).

Published by

She And The Cat's Mother

Published by She And The Cat's Mother 2017
SheAndTheCatsMother.co.uk

Copyright Zizzi Bonah 2017
All rights reserved.
Author blog site – zizziology.com
www.AliceReturnsTheMusical.com

Featured songs: 'It's Only Polony'; 'Mr and Ms'ery'; 'Sunshine In Your Shoes';
'Telephone The Ocean'; 'Monetary Girl'; 'Tush Tush'; and 'Exclamation Marks',
all written (music and lyrics) by Ida Barker.
Copyright Beatroute Records International. www.IdaBarker.live

A CIP catalogue record for this book is available from the British Library.
Paperback ISBN: 9780995747906
eBook ISBN: 9780995747913

Dedication:
To children of all ages who love the original Alice created by Lewis Carroll.

Quote:
"There ought to be a book written about me, that there ought!
And when I grow up, I'll write one –" Alice, from Alice's Adventures in Wonderland by Lewis Carroll.

Presenting

A story wherein every goodbye isn't gone and every eye closed isn't sleep, Alice must find the answer to the Looking–glass question – much to the rage of infamous book reviewer, Paige Turner who threatens to jeopardise Alice's writing career in Authorland.

Hoodlemania descends, and together Alice and her predatory blonde alter–ego, Miss Penopause walk the Critical Path to set forerunning hazards and high–jinks in motion in a bid to make Paige Turner eat her words and silence the damning book review before publication – but at what cost? For as Alice learns; it is far easier to get forgiveness than it is permission to get Paige Turner!

Contents

1

Note–a–Rioty and the Looking–Glass Question

In the middle of a hurry, Alice entered the drawing–room and came to a sweeping stop in front of the Looking–glass. "Do you know what this is?" said Alice, waving an envelope and peering round the throwback image of herself, searching for her who–went–by–the–name–of, Miss Penopause. "Oh, I really do wish you wouldn't leave the Looking–glass room as soon as I enter my dear. It is a most bothersome habit you have acquired. Though I will not be deterred, for I am quite sure you can still hear me if I raise my voice."

Alice glanced at the buff envelope in her hand. It was addressed to: Alice in Authorland. The stamp mark read: Word–sphere. Alice knew this was where the notorious book reviewer Paige Turner dwelt. And with a quiver of delicious excitement, Alice thumbed the seal open as she went on talking at increasing volume: "I must tell you, Miss Penopause, an envelope such as this contains one of two things, it is either a darling Letter–of–Recommendation, or a damning Note–a–Rioty against my debut novel!"

Unfolding the piece of paper, Alice allowed her eyes to wash over the neatly typed words. But however hard Alice concentrated, the words would not resonate to a meaning. Alice pondered over this for several minutes, until at last, a bright idea occurred to her. "Why, it's typed on Looking–glass paper, of course! And if I hold it up to the glass, the words on the paper will all show the right way round!" Alice held it up to the Looking–glass and instantly the words that were unobtainable, became obtainable to her.

This was the typed verse Alice read:–

NOTE–A–RIOTY!

Author arise to the reviewer Paige Turner,
Miss Penopause is unworthy to live,
Let us character jinx all writers with muses,
The reviewers from Word–sphere alone will survive.
Author arise and support the capital rules,
The oceans of rhyme will end words on ice,
Alice will receive excessive punctuation,
The success of a writer awaits the review.

It was angularly signed by Paige Turner.

"Riotous!" was the first word to fall from Alice's unguarded lips, but it was not long before others followed as she spoke to herself. "I must ask myself the Looking–glass question," said Alice. "And it is this – can I write without my muse, Miss Penopause? For this Note–a–Rioty states a character assassination on her. And without her, I may never have the luxury of writing creatively again!"

Alice leaned close to the Looking–glass. "Miss Penopause," she cried. "Oh, Miss Penopause, you are my fair–haired writing muse. Knowing you cannot write due to an affliction of pausing too long, is what enables me to write without pause." And as Alice went on, she barely noticed her vision into the Looking–glass was starting to cloud–over, as her heated breath hit the cool reflective surface. "Though I have never met you, Miss Penopause, I am strictly aware of you throughout my writing... In fact, I might even go as far to say the Looking–glass is the divide between myself the author, and you the story!"

And the more Alice thought, the more Alice became quite certain. "Yes, through the Looking–glass is where stories and characters live. I know this to be true as I have a vivid memory of entering that place as a young girl, though, no doubt the story has changed somewhat since I last visited. But I feel positively grand that if I was to return through the Looking–glass, I would make my acquaintance with you, Miss Penopause, and we could, together, set about finding the reviewer Paige Turner and stop her from unleashing a damning book review."

Alice re–examined the Note–a–Rioty, this time pertaining to each and every word with care, as she visualised the uncareful actions of Paige Turner. For Alice was the kind of writer who could stretch her imagination. Often she could be heard saying to her sister: "Sometimes I would prefer to see you through binoculars, then at least I'd know you'd be a long way off."

To which Alice's sister would reply, "Alice, when you start to argue that the grass should be blue, and the sky should be whitewashed as a rule, I am certain you will become a prominent fiction writer some day." But this is taking us away from Alice's speech. For this was no ordinary speech. It was from a song Alice had heard in her mind's ear when half asleep and thinking about her muse, her creative inspiration, Miss Penopause. And so, as Alice thought long and hard about the Looking–glass question, the Note–a–Rioty slipped unnoticed from her and she found herself up on the chimney–piece (though she scarcely knew how) and pressed against the Looking–glass. And she began to utter these eternal words while raising the palms of her hands against the glass, which began to dissolve away just like a brilliant shimmering mist.

Here is Alice's speech from the song, *It's Only*

Polony:–

"She tells me she has what it takes.

Oh everybody needs a lucky break.

The right time the right place.

Well optimistics have had their day.

If they believe a smile carries social sway.

"When they say people who dream too much,

Have tendencies to end up,

Cleaning out cuckoo clocks.

Well I'll reserve my opinion,

On me and you.

Cuckoo koo.

Mmm, Cuckoo koo."

And in another moment Alice was through the glass and had climbed down into Looking–glass room. "This room looks remarkably similar to the room I have just left," thought Alice. "The only difference being, everything is the wrong way round to what I am used to." She let a smile crease her face as she spotted the clock on the chimney–piece – for he was as different as different could be. "I remember you," she said with great interest.

The clock, with his old man face, acknowledged Alice

with only his minute eyes before saying: "Watch out, the face she's got on is enough to stop a chiming clock!" It was at this time, an intervention appeared through the door – a young female – who entered like a wind–dash, with her great mane of blonde hair flying and her paper clothes flapping. Alice was unseen by the female, due to the fact the female was preying upon words that were moving with great haste across her memorandum. It was clear to Alice she was using a pen to forcefully ink them down into some sort of order. But this was not going to plan as the words wriggled away. Not to be defeated, the female took a forceful stab at a word, and captured it by its tail.

"It's not easy stringing a sentence together," Alice was reduced to say at last. "Are you a writer?" The female gave out a screech and momentarily slackened her hold on the captured word; which took to running with its tail between its legs all the way into the next paragraph. "Oh, I didn't mean to cause alarm," said Alice as she soft stepped a little nearer, for Alice had seen something of a flicker within the eyes of the female. Something right at the centre of each eye. Something without a name, but which Alice was convinced wouldn't go nameless for too long. "Who are you?" said Alice, then remembering her manners she introduced herself.

"You don't look like an Alice," said the female, bringing her mane of tussled blonde hair to one side with an air of disinterest.

"As sure as the nose on my face, I am Alice and have been so since I was given the name." Alice squared her shoulders to signify she was a person of her word.

The female opened her mouth and said: "In my opinion, you look more like a... more like a like. A comparison. A simile!" And in a brief but very revealing moment, the female moved in a familiar way that provoked Alice into sudden awareness. For this was no ordinary female. This was Miss Penopause!

"You don't know me," said Alice, embracing Miss Penopause with an eagerness she seldom reserved for people. "But I know you very well."

Miss Penopause grew rigid. "Well, can I suggest we keep it that way," she said prising herself from Alice's hold.

Alice, who by now had started talking more to herself than Miss Penopause said: "I think we compliment each other exceedingly well." And as she went on, Alice surveyed her writing inspiration in a praiseworthy manner. "I knew you were blonde, Miss Penopause, whereas I have taken to darkening my hair and wearing bold colours in the belief I might appear more dramatic in my role as an author –"

"An author?" Miss Penopause's eyes grew larger and larger and rounder and rounder. "Authors are strictly not permitted to enter this side of the Looking–glass as the cost of doing so is unquantifiable, some even say they risk falling into their own story!"

Alice could not help but hear the bad colour in Miss Penopause's words, and so she felt compelled through duty to explain herself away. "It is by no accident I come here to find you, Miss Penopause it is simply a case of survival. Yours and mine, as we are creativity connected." Alice lowered her tone to signify this was a matter which carried concern. "You see, I have grave news. I have received word from the book reviewer, Paige Turner via a Note–a–Rioty."

Miss Penopause looked down at her memorandum as if it was very faraway, when it was clear to Alice it was only an every day word away. "Should I be writing this down?" Alice detected a waver in Miss Penopause's voice. "You see, I do so love to write, only the impulse seems to leave me when I can't find the correct words."

"No," said Alice softly. "I have all the words logged here in my mind. In fact, I very much doubt I will be rid of them for sometime. The memory of reading Paige Turner's indelible words will remain with me for many and a day."

Miss Penopause closed the memorandum and slid it

into her purse. The pen she artfully lodged behind one ear, as if by resting it there, it would help her hear better.

"It is no exaggeration to say," Alice went on. "Paige Turner plans to assassinate your character by way of releasing a damning review of my book, and if this happens, you, Miss Penopause will no longer exist and then I won't have a muse to write about." Here Alice took a moment to reassess her muse, and feeling her muse was not taking in the full urgency of the situation, Alice began to speak very loud and very clipped, as if she was talking to a very naughty child. "Miss Penopause, she, that is to say Paige Turner, threatens to destroy you, and my writing career!"

Miss Penopause stood quite still for a long moment and Alice thought she must be in shock. "Yes, shock," she plum rolled for. "I have heard it can effect characters in all sorts of ways."

Eventually Miss Penopause broke her own silence. "I've never been someone's muse before."

"Well you are mine," said Alice kindly. "And I intend to hold onto to you for as long as the purpose suits me." And it was then that Miss Penopause began to talk in a confidential manner. Alice leaned in to make sure she didn't miss one word.

"Paige Turner does not approve of flare you

understand..." said Miss Penopause. "And any author who doesn't abide by her rules, her ever changing rules which are modified in her own peculiar sort of way, depending on how she feels at the circumspect time, will receive a Note–a–Rioty and not a Letter–of–Recommendation. And the difference between a damning and a darling review is what makes all the difference for a writer in Authorland..."

Alice warmed to these words and made encouraging noises to goad Miss Penopause onwards. "In which case..." said Alice.

"In which case," said Miss Penopause. "We must walk the Critical Path and find Paige Turner before she releases the damning book review following the Note–a–Rioty, but it is worth remembering, Alice it is far easier to get forgiveness than it is permission to get Paige Turner!"

:

The snow was unmarked by footprints and from this white blanket, Alice watched the twisting Doppelganger woodland extend upwards. "The snow is as lumpy as porridge," said Alice, as she and Miss Penopause took their first steps on the outland, and turned their backs on Looking–glass house.

"The Critical Path appears here only on the Eve of Iptober?" said Miss Penopause. "But we must beware of movement that is neither bird nor animal, for I have heard rumours such things can press into view and take away the description of any careless wanderer. We must remain alert at all times of those dressed in dried grasses – they are Scarers, who seek to preserve the book reviewers' livelihood at all cost." Miss Penopause drew her paper clothing closer about herself.

"And once on the Critical Path, the wanderer will find the Word–sphere!" said Alice, she couldn't hold back the triumph in her voice. Miss Penopause signalled agreement. "But why do they live in the woods?" Alice looked about, as if to see the answer etched into a tree trunk.

"For the simple reason it offers protection from writers who would otherwise seek revenge against those responsible for harming their writing careers. The reviewers have chosen the woods as the woods hold great magic." Here, Miss Penopause came to a stop to add extra emphasis on her words. "Every page from a paperback is made out of pulped trees. These woods are the true origin of the physical product – a book. The reviewers themselves are from the element fire, whereby the two dominant forces that govern their characters are passion and impatience – each time a damning book review is released, a section of the woods goes up in flames –"

"And another author's career goes up in smoke," supposed Alice, as they warily trudged on into the depths of the woodland.

"Take note of smoke signals..." said Miss Penopause. "It's important to remember, Paige Turner is simply that, a page turner, not a page writer. It is up to us to find a way round the inevitable..."

Alice thought on this before saying, "I'd like to make her eat her own words!" She was surprised to hear a darkly dangerous tone in her own voice, and this one thought led into another and yet another. Thoughts that could papercut the likes of Paige Turner, yet paper–over Alice and Miss Penopause's dilemma. But for the moment, such thoughts were too precious to be shared. Alice wanted to hug them to herself a little while longer, as she allowed them to fully form in her mind.

And then it happened, the Critical Path emerged out of the white quilt, and the woodland turned and twisted into welcoming trees – whereby their boughs created an archway ahead – and Alice and Miss Penopause could see a greensward emerge – where the biting cold lifted and the woodland was transformed into the first flush of new buds, springtime.

With no words shared between them, Alice and Miss Penopause moved from the winter season and onto the greensward. Hearing giggles shimmering in the air, as their eyes came to rest on a wooden placard nailed to a tree trunk – that had no words etched into it. "Dialogue Dearth," said Miss Penopause, with the flare of one in the know.

"Dialogue Dearth?" said Alice. "Dearth means, lack of."

"It is a pointed remark by the reviewers to criticise an author's lack of dialogue, or to say, there should have been less of it." Miss Penopause inclined her head with a beautiful gesture, as if she would clean swoon away.

But Alice's mind shifted as a horrid breath pressed across her cheek, and she was left holding onto one word. The word was: who? And her eyes fleetingly saw a snowy feather dance on the spring–tide breeze, and then the owner of the feather taking position on a welcoming branch high above: the Whooie bird.

2

The Death of Dialogue

"Whooo?" called the flight creature that had stalked many an author's nightmares, including Alice's – more times than she cared to admit.

"I'm Alice and this is Miss Penopause," said Alice, then turning to Miss Penopause she spoke in a hushed tone. "I've heard about the Whooie bird. He holds great power, power many of us have no way of attaining. But if we're clever enough, the Whooie bird might part with the kind of information we so desperately require –"

"How so?" said Miss Penopause a trifle high.

"The Whooie bird only has a limited amount of dialogue," said Alice. "Now from what I can recall, if we ask the right questions – the right answers will become available to us." Alice brought a trembling hand up to her lips, not to stifle her words, but to conceal her smile. For she never thought it possible to meet such a bird as great and as wise as this.

Alice had once seen a picture of the Whooie bird in an exotic dictionary, depicting the large regal head of white, hooked beak and razor sharp claws, though she never once believed she might have the chance to speak to such a creature. And yet here she was, peering into the welcoming tree boughs, sighting the living, breathing version of the printed image. "He is a truly magnificent specimen," said Alice. And so much so, Alice dare not take her eyes from him in case he ceased to exist at all – rather like a flight passenger who dare not drop her concentration from the wings of the plane she is flying in; for fear it will surely drop clean out of the sky, should her willpower waver in the slightest.

But the Whooie bird did not keep Alice and Miss Penopause waiting long before he spoke into the concentration of silence. "Two?" he said, in a voice louder than the horrid whisper.

"Yes, just two of us," said Alice, not hiding her relief to his continued attendance. Then whispering to Miss Penopause she said, "Take note of the Whooie's answers – here, let me give you an example..." Alice cleared her throat before saying, "How should an author go about gaining a favourable book review from an esteemed reviewer?" Alice held her breath as her world narrowed down to his forthcoming answer.

Slowly, the Whooie bird's eyes began to shine a vivid orange from his snow white face, as he wisely pinpointed the question and then the answer, "Too woo," he cooed from his great height.

"I think it's a bit late in the day to start wooing Paige Turner, no doubt her review's already been drafted," said Miss Penopause.

Alice agreed while re–examining the Whooie bird's superiority. Then she came from a different angle by saying, "And how can an author prevent a damning book review being made public?"

The great bird swivelled its head 360 degrees and shone his white–tide face in their direction, and for the first time Alice felt his mesmeric stare pinpoint her very accountability. "Too wit," he said, with a degree of intention Alice could only describe as deliberate.

"I think I'm beginning to see what you mean," said Miss Penopause. "So long as we ask the right questions, the Whooie will give up his secrets."

"Hidden in plain sight," said Alice.

"Just like the Critical Path," cried Miss Penopause, for it was her turn to speak.

The Whooie bird turned his majestic head away from them to survey the Critical Path, and Alice and Miss Penopause had no intention of disappointing his foretelling words. Wit was now going to be their new by–word. "We must use wit to undo Paige Turner's damning review," said Miss Penopause as Alice's eyes came to rest on the

Whooie bird's restless claws catching the dawning greensward light, Miss Penopause had noticed too. "Is the Whooie bird safe, I mean to say, Alice, are we safe in his company? I'd hate to be taken as prey. While I came here by accident, I would like to say I stayed here on purpose."

"Quite safe," Alice reassured, her mind recalling the habits of Whooies from the exotic dictionary. "The predominate food source of such a majestic creature is the Boobook bird, primarily the eggs of the Boobook bird."

"I never knew," said Miss Penopause, raising a pencilled in eyebrow.

"Oh yes," Alice went on with her second–hand knowledge. "For the Boobook egg is the very essence of a story idea. The Whooie bird will take such an egg and devour it before a potential author exhibits –"

"You mean, egghibits?" said Miss Penopause, her eyes reflecting a warmth Alice was beginning to bathe in.

"Rather," said Alice. "Before a potential author nurtures their creativity and fully develops a storyline from its embryonic egg form."

"I don't disbelieve you, Alice," said Miss Penopause. "Here on the Critical Path, everything is related back to the process of creative writing." And a shared understanding passed between them. "Why, there must be plenty of would–be writers who fall by the wayside and never find the discipline to make their ideas fully formed," said Miss Penopause. And she and Alice saw the Whooie bird with renewed character. For he was truly living well off the spoils of Boobook eggs that writers failed to nurture.

And as if he had been found out for the creature he was, the Whooie bird pushed off from the branch above them and called out "Whooo?" And in no less than a stolen moment, nearly every branch that made up the welcoming trees came to life, with vivid eyes appearing from the depths of hidden darkness which the light of dawn had yet to touch.

And the spectacle rose into a chorus of horrid whispers, all calling out "Whooo?" Before a rush of eyes grew rounded bodies and carnivorous gaping beaks, and great wingspans stretching out across the new and changing horizon. And in no time at all, a breath of feathers of all kinds and colours flew passed Alice and Miss Penopause, pushing them off their feet and spinning them round, as Whooie and the Hooting birds swooped down and into the far depths of forest along the Critical Path. Levelling in their wake a rain of ownerless feathers dancing down to the greensward.

In breathless amazement Alice struggled to her shaking feet, but found her voice had not escaped her with all the commotion, "To stand any real chance of success, I feel we must become less obvious in this woodland," said Alice.

"I've always prided myself in standing out," said Miss Penopause, who like Alice was covered in white, brown and grey feathers.

"Perhaps so," said Alice, helping her from a crouching position. "But for where we're going I feel a makeover is necessary."

"Dolling up or dolling down?" Miss Penopause counted quickly. Almost too quickly for Alice's liking, as she tried to take in the brilliant arrival and the all too sudden departure of the Whooie bird.

"I feel we must imitate our surroundings," said Alice, gaining back clarity, safe in the knowledge words rarely escape an author such as herself. "Otherwise word may reach Paige Turner before the game's had chance to fully ignite from our imaginations."

"Oh, I do love a conspiracy," Miss Penopause enthused, as they glimpsed the last of the feathers falling.

"This is not a conspiracy. This is survival!" said Alice, wishing she didn't look quite as ridiculous as she was beginning to feel, wearing their feathered friends' cast–offs. Alice caught Miss Penopause's gleeful smile and threw one back. "Let's just make sure we're on the winning side," said Alice.

"Well, it's best to remember: A bird in hot water is nothing more than chicken soup!" This was said with a playful tone that was not lost on Alice, but Alice didn't trust herself to answer. For if she was not careful, her alter–ego could have the makings of a writer. And for now, Alice couldn't, wouldn't, deal with further competition. So, instead Alice let her eyes acknowledge her companion's existence, if not her words, as she wilfully chose to take comfort in her own personal dearth of dialogue.

3

Plotimus and Themeibus

"On me head, son," called out a voice from off the Critical Path. And before Alice and Miss Penopause had time to collect their thoughts, a vision in monochrome appeared before them breathing out hot breath.

He was a roundish chappie, Alice later said, dressed in black and white. In fact, everything about him was black and white apart from a high rosy colour on his cheeks. A colour which seemed to increase the longer Alice studied him. Quite a wholesome looking face, confessed Alice. The sort any female would be confident in seeking directions from. His baby–wide eyes hinted of emotions close to the surface. And the only flaw that Alice could see at this early stage, was a very slight twitch developing at the corner of one of his eyes.

"Would you kindly offer assistance," Alice said, inclining her head with a beautiful gesture which she had learnt from Miss Penopause. "You see, my companion and I are taking the Critical Path, how long before we reach the place where reviewers dwell?" No answer came forth. Alice debated whether he had heard her. His eye twitch was now as constant as a ticking metronome.

"My friends call me Themeibus," he said at last. "I can't say I'm particularly involved with detail. You'll have to ask my brother, Plotimus."

And before Alice and Miss Penopause could look round for this brother, who went by the name Plotimus, a voice breathed hotly down the back of their cool necks. "My brother knows his place."

Alice and Miss Penopause swung round and found themselves looking into a similar face to the first. His monochrome appearance was just as his brother's, or so Alice thought, but it soon became apparent; what was white on Themeibus was black on Plotimus, and vice versa. They were the reversal of one another. "Plotimus by name. Plotimus by nature," he said.

"What do you mean, your brother knows his place?" asked Themeibus, his twitch now increasing beyond the subtle.

"Brother, brother... we have company. Do you really expect me to lay out facts that we have already agreed upon?" said Plotimus, now sideling his way round Alice and Miss Penopause to stand in front of his kin.

"What facts?" said Alice with great curiosity.

"The fact of the matter is, plot is always more important than theme in any story..." said Plotimus.

"Incredulous," argued Themeibus, beginning to look thoroughly rubbed up the wrong way as his hands drew closer to his chest, and his nose twitched in time to his eye tick, as if to breath in some highly sensitive information – reminding Alice of an overgrown badger who had just had his lair relocated, and had found the culprit was now residing in it.

"You know it to be a truth, brother," challenged Plotimus.

"I disagree," said Alice. "One is just as important as the other for a story to be successful."

"Now, now," said Plotimus, giving Alice and Miss Penopause a judgemental look. "And what would you know about developing a story?"

"Plenty," said Alice, suddenly realising she and Miss Penopause looked more native to the woodland surroundings than she had currently felt. The camouflage of Whooie and Hootie feathers pierced into their clothing and spiked into their reworked hairstyles had indeed been more successful than realised. They no longer stood out as flagrant outsiders, instead they had linked themselves to a wing of the woodland. Still, Alice wasn't going to let their new company in on their transformation, for all they knew they could hold strong alliance to the reviewer Paige Turner. Caution must be upheld. "Balance," Alice found herself saying quite clearly. "Plot and theme go hand in hand. One cannot exist without the other. Both have their part to play –"

"You can say so," badgered Plotimus. "But some writers can't even tell the difference between us."

"And how do you tell the difference, Alice?" asked Miss Penopause looking from one brother to the other, and back again.

"Easy," said Alice. "Theme is the overall feel or objective of the story. The theme runs through the story's entirety. From first page to last –"

Themeibus budged his brother aside with his forceful round tummy. "See, I knew I had a bigger role to play than you were letting on to."

"Ridiculum!" cried Plotimus, clearly determined to stand his ground.

"Great illusions have tarnished your character, brother," teased Themeibus.

"Theme," Alice went on, while there was a break for breath between the monochrome brothers. "Theme, should be summarised in one word."

"One word?" cried Themeibus.

"One word is all powerful," said Alice, reaffirming herself.

"Oh do go on," urged Miss Penopause.

"Look at it this way, our story," Alice nodded to the current situation. And Miss Penopause mouthed the name that coloured their collective thoughts and hidden agenda – Paige Turner. "Yes," said Alice. "This could be themed as survival. While other stories maybe themed as justice, separation or even revenge. From that one word the whole story will not deviate from its theme."

"Just goes to show my importance to any story," said Themeibus.

"Whereas," Alice went on some more. "Plot is the driving obstacles that arise out of the story that prevent the theme's conclusions being reached too soon, and without trials and tribulations, obstacles and –"

"Obscenities," said Plotimus with a bitter edge.

"Those too, if the story so requires," said Alice. "Hence, theme and plot are as important to each other as yino and yango."

"Well, that's all well and good," said Plotimus. "But I have a better idea to resolve the matter." He removed something from his inside pocket, and threw, what looked like a golden pen high up into the tree branches. After a moment or two, followed by protesting bird squawks, what appeared to be a golden ball fell downwards amid rustling leaves into the palm of his outstretched hand.

"You'll never do it," said Themeibus.

"Do what?" said Alice.

"It's three against one, brother," said Themeibus.

"Brother, I am Plotimus. Obstacles abound from me. Plotimus by name. Plotimus by nature."

Themeibus leant into Alice – and Miss Penopause, determined not to be left behind – rounded the square. "First one passed the tree stump with the prize, wins. Simple as that," he said.

"And the rules?" said Miss Penopause.

"None. Just do what it takes to get the prize off Plotimus, we can pass to one another as we're on the same team. Three against one. As soon as he throws the prize into the air, the game starts. Often the first one who catches it has the best advantage –"

"Heads up," shouted Plotimus as he threw the prize upwards. And all sets of eyes flashed into the canopy of trees, searching for the soon–to–be descending golden prize. Themeibus launched himself at his brother's feet, taking him clean off the greensward, they rolled into an untidy heap to accompanying sounds of buffing and painful grunts.

"I'd wager their going to murder each other," said Miss Penopause, more than a little anxiously.

"Well, I would have said it was impossible for theme and plot to try and murder each other, but now, anything's possible," said Alice, waiting for the golden prize to head ground–ward. And as the toing and froing of the brothers guttural exchanges bruised her mind, Themeibus and Plotimus began to sing a song at each other, *Mr and Ms'ery*:–

"It's clear to see,

We are happy in our misery,

It is our security,

To supress one another's dreams.

We hold each other back,

No we would never separate,

We are each too afraid,

The other would find happiness.

"Besides you vowed,

You'd love me until your dying day.

And a promise,

Is as good as a debt.

And you're still breathing.

"It's clear to see,

We are happy in our misery,

It is our security,

To supress one another's dreams.

In some ways worse than,

Saying goodbye but then,

We left each other sometime ago,

We just never moved out no.

"Besides you vowed,

You'd love me until your dying day.

And a promise,

Is as good as a debt.

And you're still breathing.

"It's clear to see,

We are happy in our misery,

It is our security,

To supress one another's dreams."

At this moment, Alice and Miss Penopause saw a shiny, glimmering ball of hope hurtling its way into view from the canopy. Eager to make contact and hold the blessed object, Alice and Miss Penopause cupped their hands. And so it happened, the golden prize dropped straight into Alice's palms, and without second thought she made a dash towards the tree stump. "We're going to make it!" cried Alice over one shoulder.

"Don't stop," answered Miss Penopause while not a

hand breadth away. But just as they were about to touch down at the tree stump an almighty crack reverberated through the woodland, jolting their senses and stopping them in their tracks.

"Are we under siege?" cried Alice.

"Hard to tell," said Miss Penopause watchful to all sides.

Alice's nostrils fluctuated and began to fill with a most fatal fragrance – "Burning wood!" she thought. And a certain kind of dread fell heavy upon her shoulders as she spoke out into the deleterious air, "Don't tell me, an author's career has just gone up in smoke!"

Miss Penopause nodded sadly, sighting a cloud of smouldering air threatening to block out the daylight through the canopy. "The indications are all there Alice," she said. "Each tree that combusts is a tell tale sign that another author's career has gone up in smoke due to a damning book review being published."

Alice looked round warily, sighting the brothers uninterrupted fighting as close as far away. "This woodland is so highly inflammable..." she said.

"It will be an isolated occurrence," assured Miss Penopause. "The aftermath of the ignited flames belong solely to the tree they originate from, rarely do they have effect elsewhere, unless a team of writers have been involved with one book."

Alice could still hear the fatal echo resounding in both her ears. "Must have been one heck of a successful author to go out with such an almighty noise," was all she could think to say, as her eyes came to rest on the golden prize in her hands. And what Alice saw, caused her to blink rapidly as she felt the colour drain from her face.

"Are you all right?" said Miss Penopause. "Come on, let's sit down on the tree stump, you look awfully peculiar.

"Peculiar," Alice latched onto the one word. A word that did indeed summarise her feelings. "Get Paige Turner," Alice murmured.

"Of course," said Miss Penopause. "That's our whole purpose of being here." She came to sit next to Alice, and brushed the strands of hair from her companion's face.

"No," said Alice. "Get Paige Turner!" Alice moved her shaking cupped hands towards Miss Penopause. And there it was clear to see. A glinting golden Boobook egg was resting, and stamped on its eggshell in red colourant was the words: Get Paige Turner, (but as this was a Looking–glass egg, the words were reversed).

Miss Penopause's eyes dilated. "I think this may be evidence that you, Alice, have fallen into your own story. All at the cost of you entering through the Looking–glass."

Alice took a moment to register her meaning. Miss

Penopause didn't rush her. And Alice was glad of this. "Let's not limit ourselves, for could it not be possible that this is an indication of something else?" said Alice. "Perhaps we are characters in someone else's story, so to be a forthcoming book..."

"You mean to say we do not exist? We are instead, someone else's invention, living solely through their creative mind..." Miss Penopause's voice rose, and for an unscheduled moment, Alice felt quite sure, Miss Penopause would compete with her for the title of feeling unwell.

"Typical," Alice had thought. "I can't be unwell on my own for long." But with swiftness of mind, knowing this would not help their situation, Alice patted her companion's hand and spoke authoritatively. "Like any author, and I include myself here. Authors have a remarkable way of seeing a story in any given situation. Providing of course, the subject matter is more than vaguely interesting. Yes..." Alice said, feeling more like herself. "I promise you this, Miss Penopause, even if I have fallen into my own story, providing we survive this escapade along the Critical Path and reach Paige Turner, I shall write a book about it. And it goes without saying, you shall play a pivotal role." Alice saw Miss Penopause brighten up under the attention. "But first I must tell you,

Miss Penopause, of the idea that came upon me when we entered this greensward and located the Critical Path. An idea that struck me, telling me, if we are clever enough, astute enough, calculative enough, we could turn Paige Turner's words against her."

"Just like when you mentioned you'd like to see Paige Turner eat her own words?" said Miss Penopause, more than a trifle predatory, as she rearranged her paper clothing about herself.

Alice nodded. "I think we both share a talent for joined–up thinking when it suits us..." Then finding her feet and a more regular voice, Alice said, "We need to take great care and nurture this Boobook egg, if we are to stand any chance of thwarting Paige Turner by reworking her Note–a–Rioty." Alice handed Miss Penopause the Boobook egg. "And when I say this, Miss Penopause, I mean by using all the words she used, but in a different order. And in doing so, finding the opportunity to get Paige Turner to eat her own words without her even knowing it."

"Marvellous!" chorused Miss Penopause, as she placed the Boobook egg into her purse. And Alice felt like she should take a bow, or two, or oddly even three. For her re–writing of Paige Turner's Note–a–Rioty could be a story in its own right. Not the length of a trilogy, but the length needed to get Paige Turner.

4

The Rise of the Apostroflies

The pool looked as clear as a glassy lake in the misty light, and the gentle hum–humming of insects – the sort of insects that look like punctuation marks, thought Alice – danced and fluttered along the pool's surface, fanning Alice and Miss Penopause with their wings.

"I think I'll dip a toe in the waters," said Miss Penopause rather grandly, as she slipped her feet out of her paper shoes.

"You think that wise?" said Alice. "We don't know the first thing about these waters and when in doubt, I often uphold the standing to never miss an opportunity to do nothing."

"That's just your writer's imagination taking over," said Miss Penopause. "Sometimes I think you read too much between the lines, or in this case, between the ripples."

Alice inclined that Miss Penopause had made a valid point. "I tend to find of late, there is nothing more stranger than the divide between appearance and reality," offered Alice, and then on hearing a rustle, Alice's thoughts stretched out and away from her, as words struck out which did not belong to her, nor to her companion Miss Penopause.

"A writer? Oh dear me no... tell me I have misheard..." wailed the voice. "This is strictly not the kind of place to harbour the likes of a writer. Shoo, shoo away..."

Alice took a step back from the edge of the pool and peered through the leafy foliage to gain sight as to who the voice belonged to. And there sat on a rock with hands clasped to her head – as if pertaining to a wound – was a figure of a small, girlish personage. "She looks as wanton as a lily–low, and as delicate as a snow flurry," thought Alice, but as her eyes met the stranger's, the stranger signalled – through a series of rapid, jerky hand movements – that Alice should usher away. "I refuse to be shooed away," said Alice, quickly finding herself at the other side of the foliage and feeling like she had every right to be there. For as Alice saw it, this was her destiny to prevail creative integrity. And she was not in any mood to hear otherwise when she knew all routes, or to be more specific, one route, namely the Critical Path, led to the source of her problems.

The girlish stranger appeared to grow in size as her mouth appeared to reduce. "I bestow on you a pardon me," she said rather primly, as her curls fell about her fiercely unhappy face.

"I cannot have you bestowing a pardon me when I haven't asked for it," said Alice. "Where I come from, one must ask for a pardon or a forgiveness before it is given."

"You may not want a pardon, or a forgiveness, but it is yours all the same," said the girlish stranger. "This is no place for a writer, my advice to you is to use your pardon immediately by leaving this place, for if you do not, you shall insight rage from the Apostroflies and I shall be forced to grind a little more of my tooth enamel away, and I cannot afford to lose anymore teeth. No wonder I cry so much!" And she wailed on some more. But Alice, feeling neither alarmed nor moved to retreat, demanded a clearer explanation forthwith. "The Apostroflies," urged the stranger inbetween her wails and woes. "They skim the surface of my pool of tears, and at the mere notion of a writer in their locality, they will lead a swarm as big as Gerundial."

"As big as Gerundial?" Miss Penopause strode into the conversation at last. "But why do they seek out writers?"

"Because no writer can ever, all of the time, without fail, place all of the right apostrophes in all of the right places within their writings... and this above all enrages the Apostroflies who take it upon themselves to hunt such creative pen–pushers, and mockingly deposit apostrophes when and where they feel fit. It is for this very reason you must shoo, shoo away..." said the stranger with a certain kind of flourish Alice took to resent. Though she did not doubt the stranger may be missing a tooth or two by the hollowness she accented on her shoos – which gave the impression of a whistle rather than a word to be found in the dictionary.

"This is mere conjecture!" cried Alice, blinking herself back to her own personal cause and away from the stranger's advice. "I always take the utmost care when placing apostrophes within my manuscripts... and I'll even go as far to say, it is most rude to give someone advice when they have not asked for it!"

"The truth will out," said she who was not known to Alice and Miss Penopause until moments ago. "The Apostroflies have long memories, one slip up and it will be noted, two slip ups and they will begin to hum loud in protest, three slip ups and the swarm will commence once they learn of your presence here." Alice could not doubt this girlish stranger's grit and determination as she heard a little more. "But be sure, if you do not shoo away, their wrath and intent is something many of us cannot measure... nor would we want to given the alternative..."

"So what do you suggest we do?" said Miss Penopause to the stranger. "You can't seriously be suggesting we backtrack and give up our walk along the Critical Path... do you?"

The girlish figure leaned forward, and with a dismissive sob that made her curls dance and bob about her, she focused on the pool ahead. "I suggest you both get moving... you hear that hum–humming, that which is so slightly altering in pitch and speed?"

Alice and Miss Penopause took a somewhat indulgent moment to listen. And from this Alice said, "No!" You see, Alice didn't like to confess even to herself, that she was wrong. But, in a quick change of mind, the kind only females can turn on, she gave up her pride and conceded to a truth. "Nevertheless, I'll take your word for it."

And as if she'd used up her quota of words of warning, the delicate female took to her legs with a certain flighty nature and swept off along the Critical Path.

"I'm not staying round here," said Miss Penopause to Alice, quite forgetting her paper shoes beside the pool's edge. "She's got me well and truly spooked!" And off she hurried, shoe–loose.

"Well, you're not leaving me behind," cried Alice and fled after them.

Once reaching the Critical Path, the sounds of a gentle hypnotic buzzing – almost like a lure or a lulling – became increasingly louder, so much so Alice felt sure the sound had in someway located her existence on the Critical Path and was not but a few paces behind. Elevating her feet to a greater extent, Alice began to overtake Miss Penopause, and with a brief backwards glance, Alice sighted a reshaping mass of busy, buzzing, Apostroflies, dropping their deposits of apostrophes without relent!

"Move! Faster!" cried out Alice, taking Miss Penopause's eager hand and refocusing on the flighty female moving ahead of them – who suddenly grew a pair of wings and took to the air. Then miraculously a door swung open and Alice and Miss Penopause leapt across its threshold before it had chance to rebound shut, and found themselves on the inside of a room without conventional walls.

Alice's eyes were everywhere greeted by a dim glow that forced her to define the outline of her hands. "Where – are – we?" Alice was reduced at last to say as she strove to catch her breath. Aware the awful sound of tapping, constant tap tapping against the outside of the door threatened to override her attention.

"I believe – we're inside a tree truck – of all places," panted Miss Penopause. And instinctively their eyes searched for a way out, upwards. And there they saw a neat spiral stairway hugging the rounded walls.

"You know – what this means?" said Alice. Miss Penopause feigned ignorance. "Panic travels upwards, it's a well known fact in most crime writing – and invariably the outcome is not favourable – as once arriving skyward – the only alternative is down." Alice felt her outlook plummet. "Don't prevaricate!" She told herself sharply. "I'd hardly class myself as a criminal for misplacing an apostrophe or two..."

Miss Penopause steadied herself. "Well we can't stay at this level. If our means of escape is upwards, then upwards it is." She took a firm grip of the handrail, and before either of them pressed their thoughts further on the matter, Alice and Miss Penopause hurriedly climbed the exit route, urged onwards by the hollow tap tapping noises against the solid wooden door.

And their route took them nowhere but up. Up to the top of the stairs, and once there a large irregular shaped room presented itself in a warm and comforting glow. At the centre of this room stood the delicate female figure who had taken flight earlier. They noticed her tear stained cheeks had now dried. "You can call me by my name," she said brusquely. "I am known to my friends as Gramma." They politely listened as she urgently went from one side of the room to the other, checking the windows and air vents were securely locked. Alice felt obliged to do the same, aware the tap tapping was not exclusive to the door downstairs, but also the windows on this floor.

"I'll close the blinds," said Miss Penopause, feeling the need to do something, anything that gave the impression of being useful.

"And what name are you known, by those who aren't your friends?" asked Alice with great curiosity.

"Grammatical Fairidohsus," said Gramma.

"I am Alice and this is Miss Penopause, we are –" But Alice was curtly interrupted by their new friend.

"I know who are both are..." she said, indicating they each take a seat, which they did, while waiting to learn a little more about their hostess. "It had come to my attention two impostors had entered our particular kind of paradise..."

"We mean no harm..." said Miss Penopause. "Well, no harm to anyone but –" At which point, Miss Penopause opened her purse and dexterously tore off a multitude of pages from her memorandum, and within the time it took, artfully created herself a new pair of paper shoes, pinned together by an occasional feather from her head dress. "It's just as well I haven't written so much in a long while, otherwise I wouldn't have the pages to spare," she comforted herself in saying, as her interest moved back to Gramma.

"I'm well aware you are seeking her who goes by the title of a book reviewer and who dwells in the Word-sphere," confessed Gramma. "And what I can tell you is, no–one, that is to say no–body, has ever made it successfully along the Critical Path and been able to serve this particular individual the dunnyloper justice you two seek."

"Just because it hasn't been done, doesn't make it impossible!" Alice found herself saying.

"This is true," said Gramma graciously.

And Alice began to say, "I would like it to be known, authors are a particular breed should they successfully adopt diligence, determination, and down–right self-delusionary belief that they have something new to offer the already saturated world of words..." Here Alice could feel her colour coming up, so she felt it best to lay back on the subject for now, for she couldn't be sure if Gramma was for or against them.

Miss Penopause leant forward and patted Alice's arm, "Some things are too important to be cried over."

"Your answer has told me one of two things," said Gramma, moving towards the apostrophe shaped sofa. "And that is, you are here for the right reasons, but not necessarily at the right time."

Alice fanned Miss Penopause aside, not ready for

sympathy, and said in a voice loud enough for Gramma not to mistake each and every vowel: "I don't know about you, but I have met personages who are always early, and the downside to this tends to be they dislike others who are only on time..."

"Incandescent!" exclaimed Gramma, with a rush of approval that took them aback as she shoehorned herself onto the sofa between them. "You speak to the converted. Now listen very carefully," she whistled between the gaps in her teeth. "For what I am about to say is twofold, and I shall say it once."

5

Liberty Strom in the Library

"There is nothing more challenging than the challenge itself." Gramma shuffled off the apostrophe shaped sofa and presented to Alice and Miss Penopause a face deep in concentration.

"I don't see how it is possible," said Alice. "Are you really quite sure?"

"As sure as the nose on your face," said Gramma.

"And all I have to do is envisage standing outside her door, that is to say Paige Turner's door and listening for... for what exactly?" Alice tried to recall what if anything she could remember from what she had just been told. "Just the tap tap tapping of Paige Turner's typewriter, as it lasciviously embraces each damning clause and cause in turn..."

"I think it is a most wondrous solution. A solution we've been looking for all along!" said Miss Penopause, with a particular kind of enthusiasm to which Alice was not wholly sharing.

"You might think that," said Alice. "But these are not the kind of conditions I am used to working in. But then you are not a published writer, Miss Penopause, therefore you wouldn't understand!"

Miss Penopause brought her hands to her chest to signify Alice's words cut her deeply. "I do not care to participate in an exchange of crossed words, Alice," she said, half a shade flat. "I'm much more used to crossing words out, but then you wouldn't know the power of a blank page, it leaves all sorts to the imagination."

Alice wasn't yet feeling at all giving at this point, if truth be told, she was feeling rather nettled and not ready to see anyone else's point of view but her own.

"I think, Alice your creative levels require a boost of onomatopoeia," declared Gramma as she heartily extended to Alice a range of words that imitated their sounds. "Now repeat after me: Whoosh... Sizzle... Meow... Pow... Smash..."

This Alice did with some reluctance, but quickly felt ten shades brighter.

"So, just to paraphrase, Gramma..." said Alice back to her normal self. "The only way to extinguish the Apostroflies outside, is to draft a piece of work apostrophe free, or free from apostrophe mistakes..."

"Indubitably!" counted Gramma, beating her delicate wings together and causing the feathers pierced into Alice and Miss Penopause's hair and clothing, to move independent of one another.

"And you're telling me, this new draft of creative writing must be that which we must present to Paige Turner..." Alice looked for acknowledgement, and was not disappointed to receive a brisk nod of the head from Gramma.

"Shouldn't be too difficult Alice," said Miss Penopause gently. "After all, you expressed how you had thought up a writing idea to quash Paige Turner –"

Alice raised her hand to her forehead is if pertaining to new information. "Whatever happened to the superstition that every piece of writing should have two or three mistakes contained within its pages for luck money?" she said.

"Luck money?" said Miss Penopause, swivelling clean off her seat.

"Yes," Alice went on. "It allows the reader to feel an upsurge of possibilities, knowing they have caught the writer out, and proving to the reader that the writer is not all that superior to them, while at the same time, giving those readers who go by the common name of 'spoilers' something legible, or illegible as the case may be, to criticise the writer... it's all in the profession of the writing tradition. And tradition by its very nature should not be altered or tampered with... would you not agree? For no–

one likes to be presented with perfection, it's far too clinical."

"Well now," said Gramma, in a sort of droll tone, though not enough to dampen Alice's enthusiasm into certain writers' block. "Let's do keep to the facts and not waver off subject. One should always be reminded of the past while looking to the future." Here Gramma cleared her throat before she went on talking much louder than they had heard her talk before. "What you have, and we have all agreed on, is the main ingredients already. The foremost thing to place at the forefront of your mind, Alice, is this new piece has to be error free to appease the Apostroflies." She gave a generous smile as broad as her knowledge before adding: "And there is no better time to start than the present!"

"If it's not too much to ask," said Miss Penopause, in such a way to soften all but the hardest heart. "I would like to have a little input here and there, even if it's just adding my autograph at the bottom of the manuscript, you see, I have been practicing my signature off and on –"

"But primarily on!" Smiled Alice good–heartedly.

Gramma waved them through into a hidden room. "You will, I'm sure have noticed by now that this treehouse is indeed a library..." she said.

"A library?" said Miss Penopause, as if it was some

far off location she had never visited before. "But a library is usually full of books, paperback books, and here there is only a handful." Their eyes scanned the curved walls which were lined with bookshelves, yet very nearly absent of the physical product to read.

"That is due to the fact that books stored in this library are sourced from the Word–sphere reviewers, who all agreed to write a Letter–of–Recommendation," said Gramma. "And as you can both see, such recommendations are extremely rare."

"Recommendations?" said Alice, picking up the nearest books to her. "I have never even heard of these titles..."

"This does appear to be the tendency," agreed Gramma. "Books that receive blazing reviews are often only fashionable for a short period of time. After which, they rarely become in–doctored into general readership."

"So they are doomed by greatness," said Miss Penopause, as she inhaled the aroma of the few recommended paperbacks.

"Yes, often the topics and practices appreciated by the elect few are far removed from any kind of connection to mass readership." Gramma moved lightly as if not to raise the dust. "But we are deviating from the plan in hand," said Gramma. "What is paramount is this... once you have written your draft, I shall arrange for it to be validated by a Validator."

"Will you not partake in such a role yourself, after all you are Gramma?" said Alice.

"No, while I have given you the tools by way of naming the rules by which you should write with, the responsibility is yours..." she caught their eyes and shimmered exquisitely back at them. "Each Validator lives within their own validating web and shall identify any stand out grammatical errors, but the overall proof will be when Paige Turner actually samples the words from your creation."

"I'm sure by the end of this trip, I'll be able to write my own stories in my sleep," said Miss Penopause with a burst of crazed interest.

"If everyone thought like you," said Alice, "then we would simply be awash with wannabee writers, and do you know where that would leave people like me...?" Alice didn't pause long enough for her to answer. "I'll tell you where, either up a tree or down a well."

Miss Penopause raised a curious pencilled in eyebrow to their present surroundings – at the top of a treehouse. Alice gave into the absurdity of her words with a laugh they could all share in.

"There is a typewriter that lives in this library," said

Gramma kindly. "It is up to you, Alice to take the liberty and type your draft upon it as it is an exemplar authority..."

"How so?" said Miss Penopause.

"The typewriter was taken from the first ever reviewer who came to walk the Critical Path on route to Word– sphere," said Gramma. "And I do not say this lightly, but if you were to find its own innate tapping rhythm, that which aligns with the Apostroflies, there is the distinct possibility you will harness a power to disguise your true intentions towards Paige Turner... In short, it is but your best available source to the source of your impending importunity."

To this, Alice felt compelled to say: "It would appear there is not only the straight road to success, but also the straying. Liberty..."

"Liberty!" they cried as one, and at this precise moment the Boobook egg in Miss Penopause's purse rolled out and cracked open, from which a rather short, plump, yellow chick alighted, attired in a pair of painted red shoes.

"It would appear the embryotic idea titled: Get Paige Turner, has hatched into a motion," said Miss Penopause, as the chick chirped and cheeped into their smiling faces. And Gramma, insisting she would make a home for it with her, began to sing a good luck blessing to Alice and Miss

Penopause inspired by the Boobook chick's arrival.

Here are the words to Gramma's song, *Sunshine In Your Shoes:–*

"Every picture tells a story,
Into the echo of your mind.
Though the reasons come and go here.
I won't leave you behind.

"You walk with the sunshine in your shoes,
As though it's nothing new.
You walk with the sunshine in your shoes,
As though it's nothing new.

"And to your way of thinking,
Explanations take a deal of time.
But what a difference a day makes.
You won't leave me behind.

"You walk with the sunshine in your shoes,
As though it's nothing new.
Be my guide through a cinnamon afternoon,
As though it's nothing new.
The sunshine in your shoes.
As though it's nothing new."

6

The Monumoose Who Breathed New Life into Words

His voice fell just the right side of delight. "I'm a Monumoose," he said, and Alice ruminated that he dare consider saying it all over again.

"Very well," said Alice, as she and Miss Penopause touched down onto the Critical Path once more. "I'm Alice and this is Miss Penopause..."

"Alice?" he considered thoughtfully. "No, I can't say you look much like an Alice... no, more like a non–Alice."

"Like a non–Alice! Dear me, I went through something very similar to this when I first met Miss Penopause," she heard her voice rising, and quickly remembering she must not insight another bombardment from the Apostroflies – as they had taken an early curmudgeon–break due to Alice successfully typing in the treehouse – she thought it best to whisper in his ear. "And what to your mind would an Alice look like?"

"I couldn't say." He sniffed the air until his eyes shined like polished pebbles. "Perhaps a little more different. Yes, different. I'll plum for such a word as that. For as every

Monumoose knows, if you look at life differently your senses will be reawaken." He turned his handsome head to them.

"You've never looked more like an Alice to me than right at this moment," said Miss Penopause.

And Alice was encouraged to say to the Monumoose: "Well, I'll have you know I am a certified Alice."

"Certified?" he said. "That's no way to talk. You could be certified under criminal law to have your sentences lengthened in these parts, or certified to have your paragraphs evoked..."

"I hardly think those things could apply to me," said Alice.

"Well, perhaps you should. Gramma informs me you're an author, and if this is the case, then where is your sense of imagination? As a writer you do not have to have experienced all the things you write about, but you do need to have an imagination on full canter," he said all this, as if it was his sole prerogative, before adding, "Here, let me give you an example."

Alice could clearly tell from his tone of voice this would be no brief matter. Impatiently she thought it best to bring his meanderings to a stop as time was precious, and precious was time. "Oh, thank you for the kind offer, but we really must be making our way further along the Critical

Path before the Apostroflies return –"

Miss Penopause added an extra touch–truth by saying, "Yes, we have been carefully advised by Gramma that we must reach the Validator's web without delay – haste is the operate word here!"

"Say no more," said the Monumoose. "Just climb onto my back and I'll fly you both to the Validator's web during the length of my story."

"A Monumoose who can fly?" said Alice, suddenly seeing him in a favourable light.

"Imagination is limitless," he said with a broad smile that grew broader the longer they concentrated on him. And from this Alice and Miss Penopause climbed onto his back, and before they could say another word they were flying high above the canopy of trees and heading towards their next destination.

"Imagine a tree craved with words," he said boldly, as they grasped onto his brown fur and peered through his great velvet antlers.

"Craved," said Alice. "Don't you mean carved?"

"Use your imagination," he said. "Just by changing a single word the meaning can be transformed from the ordinary into the extraordinary. Is it not possible that a tree could crave words...?" Alice had to think on that one for a long moment.

"Or perhaps the tree is an object of craving?" offered Miss Penopause.

"Exactly," he said. "Let your mind open to new thoughts, new possibilities. I could say a man wore a tweet suit."

"Instead of tweed?" said Miss Penopause, entering into the game quicker than Alice.

"And the word tweet is just another way of saying cheep, meaning a sound. Leading to a variation on the expression: 'He looked sound' – allow your mind to travel, and you will find arrivals and departures less ordinary." And from these words he began to sing a song, *Telephone the Ocean*:–

> *"Telephone the ocean,*
> *Cos I heard it had a bed.*
> *Find a tide of sunshine,*
> *Cover up my head.*

> *"What if the sea had closed all day?*
> *I don't know where you said it,*
> *Ocean spray.*
> *I never read it,*
> *Ocean spray.*
> *Ocean spray.*

"And it rained all day that night.

And the past, well it fell out of sight.

And all that remains is ocean spray.

"Doors of perception,

Invade every room.

Somebody spoke,

The man jumped over the moon.

"What if the sea had closed all day?

I don't know where you said it,

Ocean spray.

What if the sand had blow away?

I never read it,

Ocean spray.

Ocean spray.

Ocean spray."

By the time Alice and Miss Penopause had landed back on the greensward they knew the Monumoose's song off by heart.

"Sometimes you have to break the rules to be noticed," said the Monumoose. "But do remember not to break the rules you make on your own terms."

"How do you mean?" said Alice, as she dismounted

with the help of Miss Penopause.

"Simple," he said, tucking his wings in spryly. "Whatever rules you make for yourself such as, a character's name, a location or even a character's description, remember not to suddenly change these rules half way through your story. It's incredulous how many author's have a character with blue eyes, who then change to the colour of blackberry." He smiled kindly and his generosity of spirit encompassed them. And for the first time Alice thought she would miss this creature of the creative mind. But instead she nodded acceptance to his words. "All I'm saying is don't break your own rules, Alice," he added.

Alice let out a laugh. "So you accept I am Alice after all?" she said.

"Well, it is the rule that you have bestowed upon yourself, and it would be wise for me to respect it," he indulged.

"Thank you," said Alice, feeling like no–one but herself.

He leant into them with his voice turned down a shade. "But tell me this, Alice why do you seek to meet Paige Turner?"

Catching Miss Penopause's look, Alice managed to throw one back as she said: "Because Paige Turner has taken it upon herself to threaten my creative writing by penning a damning book review."

"Well then Alice," his voice resounded through the woods. "That can mean only one thing..."

They waited on him for an answer, and his answer did not disenchant them. "A damning book review is a clear indication that while you may not have broken your own rules, you have most certainly broken a rule or two, or perhaps even three hundred set down by Paige Turner. But you must remember, language does not hold permanent, for over the years the meaning behind one word can and does change into a different definition. Even the academics have to reluctantly accept this fact. Though they do not take all that kindly to an individual bringing about the change, they have to accept the change when a group of individuals adopt it together." He nodded to his own words of wisdom. "Language is forever altering, and as a means of communication, I have learnt not to take words to heart, for to do so would mean waking the Thesaurus from his frequent slumber."

"The Thesaurus?" said Miss Penopause.

"Yes, he is a very old dinosaur who has had to adapt to the times of the day in order to survive modern language. Take care, he is an animal who should be consulted only occasionally, though I have known some writers, I mention no names here of course as I endeavour to be a discreet Monumoose, even if not conventional by other creatures' standards..." Here he gave a flick of his tail. "Nevertheless, some writers do have the tendency to overwork this animal." There was a faraway look in his eyes as he went on, "Yes. As I recall, a renowned literary publisher saying to his newly contracted writer: 'Now, whatever you do, do not wake the Thesaurus too often. For if you ride the Thesaurus too far through your story, you shall simply wear him out. And while I cannot afford to buy another Thesaurus, I can afford to buy another writer!'"

7

Story Gaps and the Validator's Web

With some sadness Alice and Miss Penopause parted company from the Monumoose, but as Miss Penopause kindly said, "The more you know about the past, the better prepared you are for the future." And she was right, thought Alice, for the Monumoose had now become part of their past. But before Alice could dwell on her words for any great length of time, they began to notice an irksome change taking place along the Critical Path. At first the change was barely noticeable, and then, gradually the change became all too evident as here, there, and everywhere dark shadows began to appear.

And in accordance to Alice's recollection, she fervently states she heard a din vibrating across their pathway, which Alice liken to the sound of someone clicking their tongue against the roof of their mouth. And, upon sighting silver threads of webbing floating through the air, Alice and Miss Penopause became, through no will of their own, tidily trussed up in them.

"Oh dear," said Miss Penopause, "how will I ever be able to write another word in my memorandum when I can scarcely move a step forward."

To which Alice responded by saying, "We have not come all this way, Miss Penopause, to be inked—out of our carefully drafted plan." And as if not to waste a moment longer, Alice cried out as best she could, "Hello? Heello... We appear to be stuck, could Whodunit, kindly take the time from tick—ticking and release us?"

The tick—ticking stopped. And Alice wondered whether she may regret her call for assistance, as a big bottomed female dressed in figure—hugging black, loomed into her suspicious view.

"Yes, I'm afraid we need some assistance," said Alice, in her politest of tones, hoping to bring out the other's best and not worst afflictions.

"Whodunit...? Do you know who you are talking to?" said the stranger with a mellow vibration. Alice could see this female had the most vivid blue eyes and when she closed them upon her, which she frequently did, her dark eye lashes gave one the distinct impression they had once belonged to the legs of a spider. Alice felt a shiver escape her.

"I'm afraid we haven't met before," said Alice, hoping her doubts would not betray her through her voice. "So no, I can't say I know who you are but..."

"You've mentioned you're afraid twice now," said the

stranger. "And so you should be... Though, I don't normally trap your sort of kind." She looked Alice and Miss Penopause over again as if seeing them anew.

"And what sort of kind do you normally trap," said Miss Penopause a little shakily.

"Shadow Beats," she said, pointing westward and then eastward and doing a full turn before looking at them again through her crooked long eye lashes. To this explanation Alice did not have a reply, for she had never once heard of the name Shadow Beats. "They live in the shadows," the big bottomed female went on, "and are not dissimilar to dark insects. But if truth be told, they are the shadows themselves."

"How intriguing," said Alice, feeling the silver threads tighten against her struggle to be set free. "And what do you do once you have trapped them."

"The only thing one can do," she said, as if the answer was plain for all to see. "I'm the Validator!"

"The Validator?" said Miss Penopause, suddenly looking at the female as if she was a real treat to behold. "We've been on route searching for the Validator's web."

"Well, you've found what you've been searching for," she said with approval, if not a welcome, as she began to snip and snipe away at the silver threads and release her captives.

"Oh, do tell us some more about the Shadow Beats," said Alice with relief, as she formally introduced herself and her companion to their new acquaintance. Meanwhile Miss Penopause reached for her memorandum and dabbed her pen nib on her tongue.

"This sounds like a story I'm surely capable of penning down..." said Miss Penopause, with a determined voice and a darting look.

"Call me Valerie," said the Validator. "All those who seek me out have the luxury of calling me Valerie, I find it less formal..." Then her voice changed, tarnished with conspiratorialism. "Did I mention the Shadow Beats are also known as Stealers?"

"No," said Alice. "And what exactly are they stealers of?"

"Words," said the Validator. "They feed on the words in a story and it is without exaggeration when I say, they are the most dangerous predators known to the creative mind of any writer." She paused momentarily, seeing Miss Penopause was having issues with her handwritten words as they refused to sit dutifully on the page lines. "Would you like assistance?"

"No, no!" said Miss Penopause, "They just need a little coaxing into place, nothing I can't manage..." She gave a harmless shrug as her lie temporarily became the truth.

The Validator took Miss Penopause at face value and went on. "For you see, Shadow Beats devour all meaning." She cast her webbing down onto the greensward, then began wheeling it in with a deftly hand. "It has been known for Shadow Beats to leave whole paragraphs of blankness."

"Blankness?" said Alice, her eyes taking in every movement.

"Oh yes," said the Validator. "Shadow Beats by their very existence leave story gaps."

"Tell me, Valerie, are they easy to catch?" Alice counted quickly, while noticing Miss Penopause had paused in mid–attack of turning a new page.

"They are not impossible to catch, let's put it that way," inclined the Validator. "But only the highly trained can lure them in and trap them. I myself have developed a technique whereby I have learnt to imitate the noise of a typewriter, a keyboard, the swirl and swish of a pen against paper, the scratching of chalk against blackboard... any such noise associated to setting down words onto a recording device. My results have been exceptionally good." Alice noted there was not a hint of self–effacement about her.

Miss Penopause's mouth slid to one side with a look of lost enthusiasm, and promptly slipped her pen and the memorandum into her purse. "I don't have many written words laid down," she said to herself. "But those I do have, I intend to hold onto."

"And how do you dispose of the Shadow Beats?" said Alice as she refocused on their new friend.

"My, my. You do ask a lot of questions don't you?" said the Validator.

"Well, there is no other way to ask but through a question?" said Alice keenly. Though she could see the Validator was thinking thoughts over a rough edge.

"Perhaps," said the Validator, then breaking the silence that was beginning to take hold, she added. "And how do you suppose I dispose of them?" It did not escape Alice's attention that she answered with a question as her vivid blue eyes shone bright with purpose, and her long dark eye lashes appeared to move independently from one another.

Alice thought hard. "With light?" she offered.

"No, no... that would never do," said the Validator. "You see, they, the Shadow Beats, have no substance of their own, they are merely thieves on the take. Light cannot show them for who they are and expose them. One must be much more resourceful when dealing with such beatniks."

"Well then how do you dispose of them?" asked Miss

Penopause, a trifle too high to her own liking, as she reassessed their surroundings.

The Validator did not pause for breath, "You hire a skilled Validator like myself to come along and spin webs to repair the holes in your story caused by the gorging Shadow Beats, and in doing so, the Shadow Beats become enmeshed within my web, and before long their beats beat no more." She smiled for the first time showing her irregular, but quite pretty teeth. "Won't the two of you join me for a light supper? I very rarely speak so many words in one day, and already I feel I'm sure to have used up my monthly quarter. But as you seem to be such questionable personages, I dare say I could allow you to over stay your welcome a little while longer."

"That would be greatly appreciated," said Alice, before the Validator could change her mind and take back the invitation. "What will you be serving for supper?"

"Oh just the usual," she said. "I have very apple pie manners. Besides, as you have searched me out, it would suggest to me you have a piece of written work you require to be validated?"

Alice handed over her newly typed weapon of words.

The Validator looked down long and hard at Alice's typing skills, and after a moment or two she spoke with a spike of amusement. "So you're here to make Paige

Turner eat her words," she said. "Well now, you may not be the first, but what I do know is you have to get permission last."

:

"I thought she said apple pie?" said Miss Penopause, emphasising each word with a particular ring of disappointment. "She's forgotten to add apples, not to mention sugar! And you know me Alice, I'm not a sweet toothed person, but this..." she prodded the un–appetiser round her plate. "Well, it's a real facer. And while I'm not big on words, there does seem to be only one word that can sum up this facer, and that's insipid!"

Alice turned a deaf ear to her companion, while acknowledging her own appetite had suddenly deserted her for some other time. But Alice endeavoured to be polite to the Validator, and so brought up the fork to her mouth for one last mouthful.

"Would you like another slice?" said the Validator generously.

"Oh no," said Alice with honesty. "I'm not a pastry kind of girl."

The Validator gave Alice a little pat on the hand. "I believe it is important to let you know, Alice, when one wants to attack another through the use of words, the most effective way to do so is by attacking your opponent's ideas or opinions, but never, ever, the person. For one must remember that in an attack, the attacker and the attackee are both on parade. This is something writers seemingly never learn."

Alice swallowed hard and caught Miss Penopause's eyes.

"Of course," said the Validator, handing Alice the typed work she was due to present against Paige Turner. "The aim of a story writer should be to make lives larger and more informed. Whereas attack writing is personal and seeks to cause personal damage." She broke into a wide smile. "Alice," she said leaning across the supper table . "I'm happy to say I can validate your writing. You have turned Paige Turner's words on their heads and without showing an edge of your own passion, and for this quality, you do stand a chance of making Paige Turner eat her own words."

"Do you really think so?" said Miss Penopause, pushing her plate aside. "Now you're not just sugar–coating our chances are you, Valerie?"

The Validator held her smile in place as she presented a small bowl from across the table. "Care for an almond?" she said. Miss Penopause took a handful and bit hungrily into them.

"Good?" enquired the Validator.

Miss Penopause nodded with broad movements. "Quite validating."

Alice reached to the bowl just as the Validator went on to speak. "I've never cared for almonds myself," she said. "Though I am partial to the sugar–coated ones..." Miss Penopause stopped in mid–chew, and Alice felt a prickle of something that hinted at the edible treats. "I've plenty more almonds if you'd care to have them. Always keep a store for my guests," she added. "For I have no need for them, once I've sucked all the sugar off."

The following moment was somewhat of a blur for Miss Penopause. However, Alice told her (much later of course) that her un–guesty coughing fit followed by uncharacteristic language, bruised their hostess's mind and had the immediate effect of putting an end to their supper outing.

Miss Penopause confided in Alice, she would not admit nor deny this to be wholly truthful, but would go as far to commit to memory the remembrance of waking up in an undignified heap beside the Critical Path, with a pair of eyes looking back at her. Eyes, she recalled, that held a look of shimmering mockery, in a face that was no more than a clearing in the woods.

8

Scaring the Scarers

Alice was still trying to think of something eternal to say while assisting Miss Penopause from a horizontal position to stand vertical, but in its absence Alice chose to stick to safe ground. "How are you feeling?" she said.

Miss Penopause struggled to speak clearly, but when she did eventually communicate a word that Alice could recognise, it was a word she took to mean as the end of the whole horrid subject. "Almonds," was all that was said.

And so they continued in relative silence along the Critical Path, with only the sounds of their breathing and their footsteps crushing the ground to punctuate the warm evening air that came to settle about them. But before long the relative calm was broken by movement stirring the leaves of the trees, and rushing across the grasses either side of the Critical Path. And they heard voices singing in the far distance, their lyrics Alice would later liken to the sound of a running stream that could blunt the manners of the most well–behaved.

These are the lyrics Alice and Miss Penopause heard, *Monetary Girl*:–

"We all know girls don't make passes,
At men who wear glasses.
But I was looking for a man who would,
Refuse me absolutely nothing.
His ordinariness should rather off set,
My looks extraordinarily well.
The only trouble is I haven't met him yet,
Though not through a lack of trying.

"Oh I tried lawyers,
But I never win the argument.
I've tried farmers,
But they see me as a priced cow.
And I've tried businessmen,
But they always seem,
To be, far and few between.

"I tell myself perseverance,
Is the operative word.
But it's such hard work trying to ensure,
A comfortable life through another.
His affluent means would surely agree,
With me extraordinarily well.
Still the only trouble is I haven't met him yet,
Though not through a lack of trying.

"Oh I tried lawyers,
But I never win the argument.
I've tried farmers,
But they see me as a priced cow.
And I've tried businessmen,
But they always seem,
To be, far and few between.

"We all know girls don't make passes,
At men who wear glasses.
But I was looking for a man who would,
Refuse me absolutely nothing."

Alice and Miss Penopause searched the grassy verges for they who had sung, until their sight condensed upon a cluster of dandelion clocks swaying in the breeze. Their bodies were as you would expect, tall, lean and green. And their manes of white hair framing delicate, pretty clock faces gave them the natural look of illumination.

"I wonder if you would care to tell us the time," said Alice, stepping from the Critical Path and onto the grasses.

"Tell you the time?" said a dandelion clock. "Certainly not, I've only just fixed my hair, and what I have left could be taken on one breath from this breeze if I don't angle myself appropriately." She edged this way and then that way to prove the point to Alice.

"But that would mean not living up to your name," said Alice. "You are a dandelion clock, are you not?"

"I most certainly am," she said. "But today I'm feeling vain. Not plain."

"In which case you should relinquish your name immediately if you choose not to live up to it." Alice felt her statement should not be questioned, given the fact that they had established the name game.

"Relinquish?" said the dandelion clock, and a general murmur of mutiny circulated from one dandelion clock to another as they swayed away from Alice. "And who are you, to tell me?" she said, folding her leaves about her.

"Oh, I must have dropped my manners," said Alice. "Now where did I leave them last?" She looked round and not seeing she had dropped anything in close vicinity, she offered her introduction instead by way of greeting. "My forename is Alice."

"The name Alice means nothing to me," said the dandelion clock. "Whoever heard of a plant called Alice?" And this question was repeated by all the other dandelion clocks in turn.

"Oh no, I'm not a plant," said Alice addressing them.

"I'm regarded in some parts as a social climber – a writer in fact, and my name is linked to adventurous lands that few have discovered, but many visit."

The dandelion clock narrowed her eyes upon Alice. "I once knew a social climber," she said. "Mm, went by the name of Poison Ivy, and when she wasn't poisoning by-passers, she was placing a stronghold round other plants and restricting their movements. She was the most hazardous type of climber. No, I prefer the company I keep to grow close to the soil."

Miss Penopause came to stand close by and study their new acquaintances with a fanatic eye. "That's the trouble with talking to plant life, given half a chance you'll find them uprooting the original subject, and scattering seeds into darkened places that no–one thought to talk about." Then bending low to the ground, Miss Penopause preceded to speak in a slow, deliberate tone. "I go by the name of Miss Penopause, a name that characterises who I am, so much so, whenever I put pen to paper I have the perpetual habit of pausing."

"Ah–ha!" said the dandelion clock, as if she had found them out in some far off place and had caught them red–handed, leafing through an overdue library book. "Characterisation..."

Miss Penopause stood up as straight as a ramrod.

"What kind of linguistic is that to use, and so early on in the day?"

"It's descriptive," said Alice. "But not that early, for we have already had supper."

"You forget," said Miss Penopause. "Here, through the Looking–glass the first is the last and the last is the first. Supper is always served before tea, dinner, lunch, and lastly breakfast."

"Where I come from everything is timed differently," said Alice. "But what I do know, is a dandelion clock is nothing if she does not tell the time. And as time is precious and precious is time, we, through no fault of our own seek to estimate how long we have left before we can expect to run into the most ruthless personage who goes by the name of Paige Turner..."

The dandelion clock unfolded her leaves and placed them upon her slender hips. "Plant Alice, your sense of timing is no sense at all," she said.

"That is as may be," said Alice, remembering she was sure she had her manners stolen by the rush of breeze through the trees only moments ago.

"And it's by no means an excuse to lose one's head over the matter," said the dandelion clock, reaffirming she still had a full head of hair.

"But it's not my head I'm asking to lose," said Alice.

"I'm merely appropriating the necessity of time."

Miss Penopause leaned into her companion, her voice was more hushed than normal. "Tell me if I'm wrong, Alice, but to my mind there is only one way a dandelion clock can tell you the time, and it isn't from speaking."

"Oh, yes," said Alice. "I think I have quite got into the awful habit of asking the ask instead of doing the do." Then reaching down to the dandelion clock, she said quite plainly, in case the dandelion clock was in any doubt to her meaning. "I will have to forcefully exhale on you, my dear. And the number of exhales it takes for all your hair to fly off your head and away on the breeze, will tell us the number of the time."

"For all the petals in Rosemead," protested the dandelion clock. "I have never known such obtrusive behaviour in all my life! If you knew about characterisation, you would know it is acted out through one's behaviour and desires, from the first to the last, in order to be believable."

"Here, here," said another dandelion clock just off by the thicket. "And moreover, if you intend to take the time, where exactly do you plan on keeping it?"

"Now look here," said Alice to the second dandelion clock. "I have no argument with you."

"I should think not!" protested the second. "It is most

rude to go round picking arguments with plant life when you haven't substantiated the present picking. And I maybe short–sighted, but even I can see you have no vase to place your pickings in."

Miss Penopause gave Alice a sharp nudge. "Some people believe dandelions to be weeds you know..."

"I'll have you know weeds are merely plants in the wrong place, and I'm exactly where I ought to be," said the first dandelion clock. "You on the other leaf, are exactly where you ought not to be. And I shall go further to say, if Plant Alice, you are indeed a social climber–come–writer as you so claim, I suggest, no I go further and insist, you place your aversion in writing and go through the proper roots before requesting I tell you the time."

"Did she say plant roots or path routes?" said Miss Penopause.

"I can't be sure. But perhaps she has a point," said Alice, beginning to soften for a moment. "And I do so love to write even if it is just filling out a request form..."

"Fiddlesticks! Look out!" cried Miss Penopause.

Alice jumped back against the nearest tree, for the woodland branches swayed so that leaves whirled and faces gazed down, round faces with no expression and wearing threadbare hats and frayed scarfs. And in another moment, the noise of clitter–clattering took hold, like sticks whacking sticks. And untidy creatures tumbled down from the trees, like unfetched parcels with aged overcoats tied with knotted string over faded shirts and high–rise trousers. And dried grasses peeping from scuffed cuffs.

"Scarers..." mumbled Miss Penopause through trembling fingers. "You remember, Alice I warned you about them, they'll do anything to protect the reviewers from harm's way..." The Scarers cluttered close to Alice and Miss Penopause, clitter–clattering their ligneous limbs. And their gaze excelled out of holes set within their furzy heads. And Alice and Miss Penopause could do little but listen to their skewwhiffy, for they were creatures like nothing ever written down before on this, or the other side of the Looking–glass.

"Byjingo. Pettifoggers. Pettitoes," they said. "Eebygumbowers – go-pah-go..."

And as they went on with harangue voices, a sudden thought struck Alice, yes a strike from the hands of time itself. And Alice realised the Scarers true meaning, and she gave up being scared of them as she spoke into the stolen air. "Of course, a story should speak in the voice of its characters, speak accordingly to its stripe, its experience and want. The writer's voice should not be heard. Only the characteristic of the speaker and it is for this reason the Scarers speak nonsense..."

"Characterisation, you say? That's all well and good," said Miss Penopause not feeling the benefit, "but tell me Alice, how do we scare the Scarers away? For I feel sure if they continue much longer with their tormenting behaviour, my creative mind shall never be the same again."

And the unavailable became available to Alice, as she bent and picked two long grasses from the greensward. "The only thing to do is to speak to them in their own language." And in one fluid motion Alice brought the two grasses up to her puckering lips and blew loudly, creating a vibration of noise that translated itself into their furzy heads. And from this the Scarers disappeared without so much as a what, why or a who.

"The time is exactly now!" announced the dandelion clocks with clockwork timing. And that was the right time for Alice and Miss Penopause to move forward along the Critical Path and pick up their manners from a clear stream of consciousness.

9

"Who Gave Permission?"

Under a cinnamon sky, Alice and Miss Penopause found the Critical Path had come to an abrupt stop, and in its place was a track. A rail road track.

Suddenly a great rush of energy blew Alice and Miss Penopause clean off their stride. And as they convened the courage wayward, they saw before them a Conductor descending from a tonderbus carriage.

"All aboard the train–of–thought," he shouted, and a group of eager travellers appeared from the deepest depths of the woodland and clambered abroad the carriages, bringing with them a carnival attitude as they boarded one by one.

"Wait! Wait Mr Conductor..." cried Alice, as the Conductor was about to blow his whistle. For she felt sure she and Miss Penopause must catch this train–of–thought before it disappeared. "What destination will you be traveling to?"

"Why," said the Conductor in an exquisite sort of way. "We shall travel through the district Word–sphere and round the Beauty Spot of course."

"The Beauty Spot?" said Alice, for this was the first time she had heard of such a place.

"Yes," said the Conductor, nodding his head vigorously. "The Beauty Spot is a township where the reviewers live. If you intend to have a guided tour of where these renown personages dwell, I suggest you catch this thought pronto, do you not agree?" He looked deeply compelling at Alice and Miss Penopause, as if the question alone was unusually complex.

"Oh yes," said Alice. "We long to meet and greet the legendry reviewer who goes by the title of Paige Turner."

"Ah, it is a sure fire thing, reviewers tend to have their portraits touched up, their academia touched up, but their self–made titles never touched up." He moved little in a long way. "They are a law unto themselves and must be approached with great care and planning."

"We have a plan. A plan that has been carefully worded," said Alice, feeling for the first time the end was in sight.

He looked neither interested nor disinterested, he just looked plain back at them. "I would ask you why you seek to meet Paige Turner?" he said. "But under the circumstances, I seem to have lost my train of thought while standing here talking to you." He gave a dismissive flick of the hand, as if the thought once known to him would reappear in its own sweet time. "No fuss," he said. "Let's catch the tonderbus and resume the confabulation abroad."

Miss Penopause needed no second telling. "Just as well," she said. "It's a most urgent matter we locate Paige Turner..." Then turning back to Alice. "Though for the life of me I can't quite remember why..." Alice saw a fleeting glint at the centre of Miss Penopause's eyes as they boarded.

"You're so susceptible," said Alice, and the Conductor blew his whistle and the train–of–thought was on the move, travelling the peripheral of the Beauty Spot through the Word–sphere. And every passenger had the luxury of regaining their thoughts with clarity.

It was with a fleeting stride and a revellers tongue that the Conductor informed his passengers of the wonderful delights and scenic views they travelled through. "Here on your left you will see the house of Miss Journal Lees, while on your right, you will locate the home of the reviewer Mr Crit Teek..." The passengers lurched from side to side to keep up with all the information tondered upon them.

"So many reviewers for such a small habitat," said Miss Penopause.

"Quite," boomed the Conductor. "But what else do you expect when there are sooo many authors. It is as if the reviewers live off creative hopes with mind to award only the very few, in order to keep the masses longing for their appreciation, and in doing so, elevate their own need to be recognised."

"Tell me," enquired Alice to the Conductor. "Will you be stopping the train–of–thought close to Paige Turner's residency?"

"Certainly not!" said the Conductor with an air of self–importance. "This is a guided tour, not a stop–off start–on outing. I would be stripped of all my guide–script should I dare halt the train–of–thought anywhere close to where these esteemed individuals dwell!" He heeled his leave and carried further along the carriage.

"Oh my..." called out a passenger with shrillness. "I do believe that's the reviewer, Column Inches towering above the multitudes." This comment was accompanied by gasps of excitement.

Meanwhile Alice turned over in her mind what they should do next. "Miss Penopause, I do believe we have little alternative but to jump from this tonderbus once we hear the Conductor inform us we are approaching Paige Turner's residency."

"Jump!" said Miss Penopause, as though an unsettling feeling had come to rest like an unwelcomed guest and persisted in taking up carriage space. "I feel you have mistaken me for someone else. I have never, and neither do I ever, plan to jump from a moving tonderbus carriage. Why the thought alone is preposterous. Wherever do you get your imagination from, Alice?"

"I may have an overactive imagination," agreed Alice. "But that is because I am a writer. And if we are to take part in the final undoing of Paige Turner, then I insist we jump without haste." Alice took Miss Penopause's arm and strong–held her to the nearest carriage door.

Looking out through the window, Alice denied herself the queasy feeling overcoming her as the Word–sphere rushed passed their vision in an alphabetic blur. "I see it like this," said Alice, mustering all her bravado. "I scarcely think things can get much worse if we stick to the plan, therefore how can they really be any worser."

At last the Conductor announced to his passengers. "Here on the right, adjacent to the Scroll and Ink Club is the golden doorway, of which the renown reviewer Paige Turner lives behind..."

And before Miss Penopause had chance to open her mouth and remonstrate, an insistent shove propelled her from the doorway of the moving tonderbus, to crash land on the hard ground and roll down an embankment, only stopping once she had run out of spins.

Following a long sickness came a longer elation as

Alice and Miss Penopause shook themselves back into some normality. For Alice remembered her sister saying often: "First impressions have a lasting effect." And as they were only strides away from the reviewer who had come to live in their shared creative nightmare, Alice recognised they had the advantage of forward thinking, knowing what they wanted to achieve, while Paige Turner was oblivious to their plans. At least for now.

Alice long reached to the door knocker hanging from Paige Turner's house. The knocker was a solid golden book, but upon being reached for, it jolted into a flurry and fluster of movement as its golden pages flicked open. Startled, Alice and Miss Penopause were even move amazed to sight within the golden book, a bookworm had made its bed and was lying upright, suspended by his nightcap that was attached to an etched paragraph. The bookworm proceeded to open his heavy eyelids and pull his sleeping bag higher about himself in a defensive gesture. "D–D–Do you mind?" said the bookworm. "I d–d–don't take too kindly to being w–w–woken."

"Oh I am sorry," said Alice. "I didn't realise you were real."

"Real?" said the bookworm. "Well, whoever heard of an unreal b–b–bookworm. The thought alone is simply non–sensical."

"You look as though you've been asleep for months," said Miss Penopause, moving closer to examine this grouchy creature. "In fact, I'd go further to say you've been asleep a whole winter of months."

"You g–g–go somewhere near to the c–c–correct time," said the sleepy bookworm, and for the first time he acknowledged a pressure of eyes looking back at him. "We don't have many visitors here. And the m–m–more I think about it, the m–m–more I can't remember a single one."

"Well you have a visitor now," said Alice. "Two, to be exact. We are here to see Paige Turner."

"This is a very circumspect comment," said the bookworm. "Very c–c–circumspect indeed... in which case I must ask you who gave you p–p–permission?"

"Permission?" said Alice, who didn't like the sound of that one word. Then with the ingenuity of a writer, she decided to drop the per but keep the mission. "P–P–Perhaps, you mean to say mission?" said Alice, momentarily picking up the bookworm's stammer, not in an unkind way of course, it was just that Alice found his stammer a shade contagious. And in the next thought she wondered if the bookworm was accentuating his stammer, in order to appear more authentic and colour his rather plain looking features.

"Mission, yes, quite right. We are here on a very important mission," said Miss Penopause in support of Alice, then adding in the same breath. "Forgive me, Alice but didn't the Gramma fairy give us a pardon which we have yet to use?"

"Well, why didn't you s–s–say s–s–so in the f–f–first place," said the bookworm. "If you are here to deliver forgiveness by way of a pardon, you must enter through the tradesmen's entrance." He gestured over there, somewhere. "This main entrance is to be used s–s–solely by her who lives here and no–body, that is to say no–body else."

"You mean Paige Turner," said Alice.

"Well who else could I p–p–possibly mean?" And upon these words he closed his puffy eyelids tight, drooped his mouth wayward and began to snore more than just a little loudly, as the golden book pages whipped passed their eyes to conceal its lodger once more.

Miss Penopause took Alice's arm. "You simply couldn't make him up could you... I feel quietly sure if I was to write him as a character in a book, he wouldn't make it passed the first draft."

Arriving at the tradesmen's entrance, Alice and Miss Penopause found themselves standing among a gaggle of individuals. Now I say individuals, simply because, as

Alice told her sister later, these individuals were quite unlike any individuals she had ever met before, and that was taking into account their meeting with the Scarers earlier. But Alice insists, upon closer incursion it so turned out these individuals where living, breathing scrolls. I mean, whoever heard of such creatures. But scrolls is what they were. And Alice assures her sister to this every day, they all went by the name of Page Perfect.

Each scroll had heavy rounded shoulders from where the scroll unravelled, and this heaviness was balanced out from a similar shape round his ankles, with a hemline that rested above his two feet that pointed out at particular angles – angles, Alice described, as a quarter to three, just as the clock strikes. And as one might guess with these two feet, each scroll had the luxury of two hands which balanced a particular waddle as they moved across the courtyard and through the tradesmen's entrance. And not forgetting, to top off their heads, the scrolls were adorned with a hard–hat, which Alice couldn't help but notice grew a strong resemblance to that of a pen lid.

Now it is of the utmost importance that I convey to you that each scroll had words written across their scroll body. These words, it so turned out, were the words selected by an author's publisher, which showed the most dynamic page within each author's due–for–release book – hence the most perfect page was to be shown to Paige Turner, who upon inspection would approve or disapprove each scroll, and from this, Paige Turner would forward a Note–a–Rioty or a Letter–of–Recommendation on each Recommence Day.

After familiarising themselves to their new surroundings, Alice and Miss Penopause approached the orderly queue of scrolls. "I can't help feeling out of place here," said Miss Penopause, her voice giving way to apprehension, for she'd never seen so many written words before.

"Don't be so easily upset," said Alice sternly. "If you were as predatory with other things as you are when chasing words across a page, I dare say you would be too unruly. Just remember, everybody has to be an expert over somebody else. And the way I see it, it's good manners to present a little proof before you take the pleasure."

"If I knew what that all meant, I'm sure I'd feel a whole lot better about myself," said Miss Penopause all of a quiver.

"Just think of yourself as an exclamation mark," said Alice. "You are a statement, and the statement alone should not be questioned." From this Miss Penopause brightened up somewhat. "Now, I need your pen, but not your memorandum," said Alice. Miss Penopause obliged without delay. Then looking towards the nearest scrolls, Alice made her selection and spoke quite clear and deliberate to her chosen one. "Now, dear me scroll, what a fearsome mess you look. Here, allow me to tidy you up so that you may be a perfectly presented page for Paige Turner." The scroll, having no chaperone to speak of, turned to Alice in a pleasant sort of way. Alice vigorously rubbed one of Miss Penopause's paper shoes against the scroll and wiped him free from all his words, then Alice began to write – in reverse, for this was a Looking–glass scroll – the words she had typed while in Gramma's treehouse all that time ago, and which the Validator had approved.

With a gracious tilt of the head, Alice stood back to admire her handiwork. "There, there," she said to the scroll. "You have never looked more Page Perfect than you do right now." And with that, Alice and Miss Penopause accompanied their re–written scroll through the tradesmen's entrance.

10

Get Paige Turner

On the inside of the great golden house of Paige Turner, Alice and Miss Penopause's eyes where greeted every which way by rapid movement. Each scroll was allotted a number, and assisted by a grey looking administer up and onto a long bench. It soon became clear to Alice and Miss Penopause, that this long bench was a stationary conveyor belt, that winded its way up to a platform which displayed a large empty orange chair.

The scrolls dutifully did as each grey administer directed, and laid belly up with only their feet, still angling at a quarter to three, showing where one scroll ended and another began, all the while singing a song called, *Tush Tush*:–

> *"My author impresses upon me,*
> *I am a most perfect page,*
> *Not, just a little bit,*
> *More, like a lot of it,*
> *On this Recommence Day.*

"My author's imagination,

Reaches the curb in the sky,

Not, just a little bit,

More, like a lot of it,

On this Recommence Day.

"On this Recommence Day,

Paige Turner might say,

She loves me very, very much,

And roll me over and say it again.

"My author impresses upon me,

I am the most perfect page,

Not, just a little bit,

More like a lot of it,

On this Recommence Day."

"What a most curious arrangement," said Alice to Miss Penopause as they moved themselves discreetly behind a very tall pillar.

"I cannot for the life of me admonition what is going to happen next..." said Miss Penopause. "Though I feel sure if I were to blink, I will miss something of someone somewhere."

Alice suddenly became aware of their surroundings

picking up and moving. That is to say, the pillar moved and they, Alice and Miss Penopause, ushered after it. It was only when the pillar began to speak, did Alice realise what was going on. "Sigh–lence in the assembly," hollowed the pillar, oblivious to its two erroneous companions behind. "My name is Column Inches and I can announce Recommence Day is of the time!"

"Column Inches?" muttered Miss Penopause. "Isn't that..."

"Yes," said Alice, picking up the thought where Miss Penopause had dwindled off. "He revels in Paige Turner's judgement and writes column inches in newspapers." Alice looked upwards and estimated him to be well over ten feet tall. And as Alice's eyes shimmered across towards the grey administers, it was by no exaggeration to say, every administer straightened their backs, pulled in their tummies and wordlessly challenged to reach Column Inches towering height.

In contrast, a happening at the door presented itself, whereupon a rather stout, red haired young female with jangling bracelets, stomped flatfooted onto the raised platform, wearing a gold power dress, and upon her flaming hair a gold pork pie hat; its pastry crust in the shape of a crown with a contrariety of large gallinaceous feathers spiking the inharmonious air. She surveyed the room with bold intelligentsia before squeezing herself small onto the orange chair, which bravely creaked and stained with screams of malevolence. But the female merely dug her heels into its upholstery to show she was a person not to be moved. "This is Paige Turner!" thought Alice, giving Miss Penopause a knowing look and pulling her into a fixed shadow of safe remove, as they watched Column Inches glide his way towards the platform, coming to a stop once beside the newly occupied chair.

With a little efficient clip of the hand, Paige Turner pinged a bell and the conveyor belt sprang into action. The first scroll moved to a stop beneath Paige Turner's bulbous gaze. Column Inches handed Paige Turner a pitch–fork and a cutting–saw. And with one volatile movement, Paige Turner pinned the scroll to the conveyor belt with the three–pronged instrument – the scroll gave a squeal of terror. Alice and Miss Penopause brought their hands to their ears. "She is merciless," thought Alice, staring at Paige Turner's jagged movements as she cut a corner of the scroll clean away.

"Don't dispute with me!" blazed Paige Turner to the scroll.

The scroll could do nothing but quiver and shiver as Paige Turner brought up the ladened fork to her nose. Her nose, both Alice and Miss Penopause noted, twitched effervescently. "I detect an aroma of sentimentality... yes, rather self–effacing." She glowered with not a twinge of self–consciousness as she expanded a disproving look at the forkful, before dipping it into hogwash sauce. And taking a huge disrelish bite she closed her lips round the written paragragh on the fork, and began to chew with the power of hodge–podge justice.

Alice and Miss Penopause held themselves together remarkably well as they compressed the urge to scream in tune with the poor scroll. Miss Penopause whispered into Alice's ear. "Is this really how reviewers test out an author's creative writing?"

"It would seem so," said Alice, and sighting their scroll she added: "But just you wait until Paige Turner eats her own words. I'm perfectly sure this will make all the difference to her unsightly behaviour. All the difference indeed."

Paige Turner broke into their forward thinking by speaking her mind. "This scroll is written with flourishing swirls that I demand the author tames. A most disappointing effort." She jabbed a finger at the scroll – who not quick enough to react, found himself rolled up by the swift hands of Column Inches and slotted into a pigeon hole labelled: Note–a–Rioty.

"I think – Paige Turner may have – big–dame–

syndrome," wheezed Miss Penopause. "You know – too big to do the little things – when really she's too little to do the big things."

"She's probably just a frustrated writer," said Alice, more to herself than to her companion. "They get everywhere. Perhaps Paige Turner's motto is: Do not attempt to improve anyone, especially if you know it will help."

Time passed, and the damning pigeon holes were filling up to such an extent that they threatened to be overfilled. The restless pigeons cooing within the holes were looking as ready as ever to take flight and deliver the Note–a–Rioties to their instructed destinations. But the bell pinged again and again, indicating yet more taste testers, and such comments from Paige Turner followed: "Too heavy handed with adjectives, NEXT!" or "I call this piffle writing! It is mere typing!" or "Someone should tell these so–called authors that if they're told it would make a great novel, invariably it will NOT!"

At long last Alice and Miss Penopause's scroll came to the attention of Paige Turner. "I dare not breathe for thinking I may effect Paige Turner's concentration levels," whispered Miss Penopause as they teetered to the edge of the shadow. It did not escape Alice that Paige Turner carried a mild look of surprise as she set to tattle their scroll. They fixedly watched her lips condensing from their usual slackening, to a thin, drawstring pull, which resulted in an uncharacteristic curl of the mouth. The kind of curl that wasn't contemptable, but showed more than a hint of something that pleased her. This, Alice was quite certain.

Paige Turner cut deep into the scroll for a sample, but the scroll did not scream like those written in the style of crime fiction, nor did it giggle like those written in the style of comedy fiction, and neither did it give out a delirious sigh like those written in the style of romance fiction. It simply remained silent. Indicating it was a factual piece.

Paige Turner breathed in the scroll's fragrance and began to speak in an unusual softened voice. Almost dreamy. "I feel a sudden... how do I explain it... nostalgia," said Paige Turner. "Just the right amount of seasoning, punctuated by meaning." She took an eye–wash sample of words from the fork and began to chew.

The first chew was slow and deliberate, and from this she excelled to a fast chomping. And before anyone could have demanded second portions, Paige Turner cut into the scroll with great exuberance. The sort of exuberance Alice and Miss Penopause had not seen until now.

"Yes... Yes..." went on Paige Turner. "This is THE most original and yet familiar taste in the same mouthful... Why, I feel certain I have tasted a winner, a sure fire darling. Oh my, this is truly a Page Perfect scroll that will undoubtedly have the written approval from me, Paige Turner!" Grunting through mouthfuls of words she demanded Column Inches's full attention, "Call the Word–sphere luminaires and let them know of this great news..." And within moments the whole of Alice and Miss Penopause's scroll had been completely devoured by a greedy, guzzling Paige Turner. "I want the rest of this creative writing from the author to be forwarded to me in half a shake's time – do you hear me?!" Then with a faraway look in her eyes, Paige Turner said with more than a twinge of envy: "I only wish I had had the foresight to have written it myself."

And this was when Alice and Miss Penopause seized their opportunity and stepped across the edge of shadow. "Paige, Paige Turner? I demand your undiluted attention!" hollowed Alice across the assembly room.

There was a sharp to the taste silence. A silence Alice took comfort in, while Paige Turner looked momentarily out–of–sorts. "Gate crashers," spluttered Paige Turner to the right of her. "Gateway crashers!" she strained to the left. And reconsidered shouting some more, only she needed a glass of Read–It wine from an on–hand frog footman in order to clear her throat – which she did – swilling down the last of Alice and Miss Penopause's Page

Perfect scroll. By which time Alice had climbed onto the platform and had begun addressing Paige Turner some more.

"We have an announcement to make to you, Paige Turner," said Alice, not hiding the revelry in her voice as she lent Miss Penopause a hand and pulled her onto the platform beside her.

Paige Turner narrowed her judicial eyes on Alice as if to located her exact moment of conception. "Do I know you? I feel I have been aware of your sort before. Who are you who dare to tread upon my Recommence Day?"

"I am coming to just that," said Alice. "If only you will be patient."

"Paaaaatient?" said Paige Turner in one long breath as her voice rose in pitch and she stretched herself up and off the high–chair. "Who – gave you – permission to enter here – and speak AT me? Me – who is used to speaking AT others – not being spoken AT!" Paige Turner savagely gulped down the last of the wine then threw the empty glass at the nearest frog footman.

Alice went on speaking her long–practiced words of thought: "Has no–one ever told you, Paige Turner that kindness is inclusive, whereas envy is exclusive?"

"What? What is this language she speaks AT me?" Paige Turner looked haughtily round for someone to provide the answers. "Toxic words, she ought to be marginalised..."

"Piffle–poffal," said Miss Penopause suddenly finding her voice. "This language you hear, Paige Turner is the language of the authorpreneur, and you have been found out for the gormandiser you are!"

Paige Turner gave a perfunctory cough.

Alice went on. "The scroll you have just consumed is indeed faithful to the damning book review you plan to release against myself, Alice and my muse, Miss Penopause..."

Paige Turner took to blinking rapidly as she tried to formulate Alice's words into some kind of meaning. "And I am pleased to inform you," said Alice rather grandly. "That the words you speak so enthusiastically about, are indeed your own!"

"My own?" expostulated Paige Turner. "How incredulous, you come here and state AT me..." She clenched her hands into tight fists and thrust them down by her sides as though she might start a Rondabellyanna jig. "Do you not think I would recognise my own words?"

"I'm sure you would," said Alice. "But I placed them in a different order to disguise this very fact!"

"Hullabaloo, you are but fools! Do you know what you are saying and the fallout that it would insight? Why, I'd be sure to choke on them!" said Paige Turner as she clutched at her own throat, and then her chest. And Alice suspected a slight heartburn might be overcoming the reviewer.

"Oh yes," said Alice working in a few darkened tones. "And there is no anecdote to eating your own damning words!"

Mortified, Paige Turner rasped with amazing bad grace to Column Inches, "And what use are you to me, why haven't you disposed of these encumbrances which talk AT me? Why, you're no more use than a chocolate teapot!"

Shocked into a loud silence, Column Inches's delayed response was to start singing at Paige Turner, much to her expanding annoyance.

This is the song he sang, *Exclamation Marks:–*

> *"When you talk to me with,*
> *Exclamation marks,*
> *I know it's over but I can't,*
> *Stop loving you.*

> *"It's too late we've turned out,*
> *The lights in Blackpool.*
> *And a lie can only exist,*
> *Where there is truth.*

"For the love we came to know,
Won't bridge the gap between our minds,
Oh no no.

"When you talk to me in,
Exclamation marks,
I know it's over but I can't,
Stop loving you –"

It was rather unfortunate, thought Alice, that Column Inches had not the chance to sing the second verse, as the object of his affection bamboozled him – by throwing the nearest frog footman at him. "How typical of a male in a crisis – can I not have this ALL to myself?" cried Paige Turner, jumping up and down on every other syllable she spat and spluttered. "This is not about you, Column Inches. This is all about ME! ME, ME, ME!" Then turning to Alice and Miss Penopause, Paige Turner managed to say: "And I swear you two are as rare as a row of turkeys looking forward to Christmas!" before submitting to another round of unscheduled splutters, punctuated here and there by a cough – a cough that grew larger and larger and rounder and rounder.

"It is most rude to cough over someone else's words, has no–one ever told you so?" said Alice, for she had not finished her reprimand speech.

"I'm not coughing," gasped Paige Turner, who's face was now turning the same colour as the orange chair. "I'm choking!" And as the choke went on to shake and break and wake the walls, it was only dampened by the pigeons who began to claw away at the Note–a–Rioties, so much so, that an unprecedented flurry of paper confetti began to shower down and blind everyone's vision. And within this movement, the paper confetti began to shimmer and glimmer and shine.

"Oh," thought Alice, "this is just like looking into a Looking–glass. Highly reflective. And if I look through my eyes and narrow my gaze until it becomes quite exact, I could swear this is in fact a Looking–glass, which brings me in mind of the Looking–glass question. And suddenly I know the answer!"

And as Alice contemplated these thoughts again, she found herself feeling disorientated by the storm of confetti, and she felt herself falling... falling out of the story and leaving the place she had come to know – the place where Miss Penopause lived – the other side of the Looking–glass.

11

Alice in Authorland

"Alice," insisted the kind voice. A voice she knew well and recognised belonged to her book publicist, Telus Agen. "Alice, your public are waiting for you. Waiting for you to read them the opening extract from your debut novel."

Alice blinked herself awake and focused on where she was: curled up on the great arm–chair in the drawing–room. And in another moment, Alice took to her feet and edged her way towards the clouded over Looking–glass. "I feel sure you're there, Miss Penopause," she whispered, raising her palm against the thoroughfare glass. "But was I part of your dream, or were you part of mine?"

No answer came forth. But there was a dull movement on the other side, and Alice sensed it was Miss Penopause placing her hand against Alice's palm to join their divide.

"All that Looking–glass needs is a good polish to bring out its once illustrious self," said Telus Agen, but Alice barely heard him as she leaned away from the Looking–glass and witnessed a change taking place within the framed throwback. A change which signified the confetti was clearing away, and in its place Alice could see Alice.

"Miss Penopause," Alice said to herself. "You have been along with me through the Looking–glass question, and I wish you to know, in answer to the question: Can I write without you? My answer is: I am certain I could not, nor would I ever want to be a writer without your influence." Then, reassessing the drawing–room Alice said, "Telus Agen, have you seen the Note–a–Rioty. I'm sure I must have dropped it in here before I left for..."

"Note–a–Rioty?" he said, as if the phrase was incoherent to meaning. "There's no Note–a–Rioty, but this has just arrived..." He reached into his inside pocket and handed Alice a letter. "A Letter–of–Recommendation," he said more than pleasantly pleased. "You've been tipped to make the bestsellers list in Authorland!"

Alice couldn't help but spill relief tears down her cheeks, that plopped independently onto the letter of praise.

And Alice relived this moment again and again, when reading from her follow–up novel, telling of her adventures along the Critical Path and travelling to the Word–sphere with her companion, Miss Penopause. And she was sure to recall the contents of the Note–a–Rioty penned by Paige Turner, and how she, Alice had skilfully rearranged the words.

Here is a reminder of the Note–a–Rioty verse in praise of Paige Turner, which threatened to cause the character assassination of Alice's muse, Miss Penopause:–

NOTE–A–RIOTY!
Author arise to the reviewer Paige Turner,
Miss Penopause is unworthy to live,
Let us character jinx all writers with muses,
The reviewers from Word–sphere alone will survive.
Author arise and support the capital rules,
The oceans of rhyme will end words on ice,
Alice will receive excessive punctuation,
The success of a writer awaits the review.

Now, if you separate each line into two, and read the verse as set out below, you will see exactly how Alice turned this disadvantage into an advantage, and succeeded in getting Paige Turner to eat her own words, by creating a *Two Sided Verse*:–

SIDE ONE
Author arise to,
Miss Penopause.
Let us character jinx,

The reviewers from Word–sphere.

Author arise and support,

The oceans of rhyme.

Alice will receive,

The success of a writer.

SIDE TWO

The reviewer Paige Turner,

Is unworthy to live.

All writers with muses,

Alone will survive.

The capital rules,

Will end words on ice.

Excessive punctuation,

Awaits the review.

12

Jamboree

A final word – Alice insists she has heard from Miss Penopause since their escapade together, and can announce her predatory muse has taken up writing flash fiction, therefore not posing a threat to Alice's success as a novelist.

Here is Miss Penopause's most recent attempt at storytelling called, *Jamboree*:–

The pages would not lay flat. The words impossible to read. The dark lines supporting swirls of pen marks were all moving with long reach. I leaned across the table. 'Look! Here, words,' I said. But their movements did not cease across the crumpled pages sliding into shadowy depths.

With astonishment I had to admit, they moved faster than anything I had written in some time. And as the words continued to unravel, I was sure they would lose all meaning to what I had inclined. I felt a sudden moment of... well, something I could not name, but could only be described as darkly dangerous and unnecessarily vain – for certain my written words were rebelling against me. Me, their author. Without shame!

With a critical eye I witnessed, my written characters all plotting against me. Some hiding within margins, others re–writing conflicts and solutions. And then I caught sight of the remainders, fleeing the page boundaries. It all became too much, I let out an expletive of rage.

Then taking a grip of myself, I remembered the myth between the lines. A myth which goes some way to say: if a writer suffers penopause while creating a storyline, it has been known for the story pages to contract together, allowing words to escape into the story's shadowy depths, and follow their own natural twists and turns. Meanwhile, the writer can do nothing but observe. Only carry a hopeful look to take the pen without pause, and write the story created within the story's depths.

Now I can say, while not feeling at all quite like myself – having learnt I harbour tendencies of resentment, more than a good most I suspect – I immediately wrote a new piece of work. It tells the story of word spirits, trapped within the story's shadowy depths, unable to re–enter and cross the *lines due to an author, wilfully killing them with a question mark? I would read you the first draft, only the pages won't lay flat.*

Your tarloora friend,
Miss Penopause

THE END

Thank you for reading

Alice Returns Through The Looking–Glass

13

Who's Who in Alice Returns Through The Looking-Glass?

Alice: A resplendent author who lives in Authorland, she returns through the Looking-glass and falls into her own story; all at the cost of seeking the answer to the Looking-glass question.

Miss Penopause: She is the alter-ego and writing inspiration of Alice, who lives on the other side of the Looking-glass. Miss Penopause doesn't find it easy to string a sentence together, and forcefully inks disagreeable words into her memorandum book, but they often wriggle free, leaving Miss Penopause with many unruly paragraphs.

Paige Turner: Alice receives Note-a-Rioty from Paige Turner – the frightful book reviewer – and learns she threatens to destroy Miss Penopause, by publishing a damning book review against Alice's debut novel.

The Whooie Bird: A majestic creature who glides along the Critical Path. He reveals through selective dialogue, how Alice and Miss Penopause should wit, not woo Paige Turner, to make her eat her own supercilious Note-a-Rioty.

Plotimus and Themeibus: These two quarrelsome brothers refuse to agree who is the more important in any story – plot or theme – before singing "Mr and Ms'ery" to Alice and Miss Penopause.

Gramma: A rather rude female when first encountered by Alice and Miss Penopause, on account of her dislike for writers who overlook the rules of grammar, forcing her to grind a little more of her tooth enamel away.

Apostroflies: Vengeful insects who deposit their waste onto any writer who misplaces apostrophes.

The Monumoose: A creative creature, he encourages Alice and Miss Penopause to "Telephone The Ocean".

The Validator: A different character of a difficult nature when provoked into dropping her Apple Pie manners.

Dandelion Clocks: They can often be heard proclaiming, "Today I'm feeling vain. Not plain."

Column Inches: A ten foot tall journalist who sings a melancholy song called "Exclamation Marks".

How many whimzical facts do you recall of Alice Returns Through The Looking-Glass? Take this quiz and find out how much of an Alice whizz you are...

1) Where does Paige Turner live?

2) How often does the Critical Path appear?

3) What is the relationship between Plotimus and Themeibus?

4) Why does Gramma speak with a whistle?

5) How do Apostroflies attack writers?

6) According to the Monumoose's story, why should you never ride a Thesaurus too far through your story?

7) Which creature states she has Apple Pie manners?

8) Why does the Dandelion Clock refuse to tell Alice the time?

9) How does Alice scare away the Scarers?

10) Can you name the piece of writing penned by Miss Penopause?

Answers to the whimzical quiz – how did you fare?

1. In Word-sphere.

2. Only on the eve of Iptober.

3. They are brothers.

4. She has one too many teeth missing.

5. By dropping deposits of apostrophes upon them.

6. Because you shall simply wear him out, of course!

7. The Validator, (also known as Valerie).

8. Because she'll lose her head of hair.

9. By blowing between two long grasses.

10. Jamboree.

>> Look out for the audio book!

This original story by Zizzi is also available as a screenplay and a stage play: both formats are adapted by Zizzi Bonah; script editor Gwen Hullah.

Alice Returns Through The Looking-Glass: A Musical Vaudeville Screenplay,
eBook ISBN: 978-0-9957479-3-7
paperback ISBN: 978-0-9957479-2-0

Alice Returns Through The Looking-Glass: A Musical Vaudeville Stage Play,
eBook ISBN: 978-0-9957479-5-1
paperback ISBN: 978-0-9957479-4-4

AliceReturnsTheMusical.com

14

About the Author

Zizzi Bonah is a 5ft 3" lass born of Yorkshire parents. She spent 7 dedicated years; 3 busking her self–penned songs on Bridlington, Scarborough and York streets, to then gigging pubs and clubs in and around the North of England, gaining airplay on BBC Radio York and Humberside using her birth name, Ida Barker.

A change is as good as a reply, (a line taken from one of Ida's eclectic–electric songs). With this in mind, she chose a new direction – to become a fiction author by releasing her debut novel, *#Entrangement: Where Colours Don't Bleed*, in March 2016, and a collection of short stories and verses, titled: *#GirlRogues – Braggadocio*.

In memory to the author's late grandparents – Ida (maiden name Bona) and Tommy Hullah who farmed within Nidderdale – Zizzi's nom de plume came about – merging Bona and Hullah into Bonah.

Alice will return again...

15

_______ *Your Invite!* _______

Become a BonBon Heart by following Zizzi Bonah's blog site – packed with:

SPOT IT – Tips for creative writing and internet know–how as told to Zizzi by her water vis–viva.

SCRIPT IT – Post your comments and pics all things rogue and non–rogue.

SCROLL IT – Read Zizzi's early extracts.

SHARE IT – What draws you to fantasy books?

To receive a hearty splice in your inbox click "follow" at:

zizziology.com

AliceReturnsTheMusical.com

www.ingramcontent.com/pod-product-compliance
Lightning Source LLC
Chambersburg PA
CBHW021023120726
47905CB00009B/3157